UNWIN HYMAN SHORT STORIES

OPENINGS

INCLUDING FOLLOW ON ACTIVITIES

EDITED BY ROY BLATCHFORD

Published by
UNWIN HYMAN LIMITED
15/17 Broadwick Street
London W1V 1FP

Selection and notes © Unwin Hyman Ltd, 1982
Reprinted 1984, 1986, 1987, 1988, 1989

British Library Cataloguing in Publication Data
Unwin Hyman short stories:
    I. Openings
    1. Short stories—English
    I. Blatchford, Roy
    823'.01'08   PR1309.S5

    ISBN 0 7135 1336 5

Printed and bound in Great Britain by
Billing & Sons Ltd, Worcester

Contents

Introduction

The eleven short stories in this volume have been chosen as suitable for middle school and lower secondary school pupils. First of all, they should appeal as good plain story-telling, but they also deal with a variety of ideas, subjects and situations on which pupils should be encouraged to reflect, and to use as starting points for writing their own stories and plays.

The stories are not grouped thematically but an idea encountered in one can certainly be linked with another; there is no need to move chronologically through the collection. For example, *The Holiday, Harold, Bella* and *Gaffer Roberts* could be taken together as semi-autobiographical accounts of children growing up in particular regional environments. *The Outside Chance* and *The Monkey's Paw* are fine examples of tales of the super-natural, while *How the Tortoise Became* and *Swollen-Foot* carry the reader into the fascinating worlds of creation myths and ancient legend. *In The Middle of The Night* and *The Wild Geese* might be read alongside one another as marvellously warm and atmospheric tales of childhood pranks and the ever-waging battles between parents and young children. The story *Equal Rights* (previously unpublished) will prompt readers to think about themselves, and attitudes in society today.

The Follow On section includes some simply-written notes so that the teacher can help pupils discuss and appreciate the short story genre, together with various discussion and writing points and supporting material to take readers into and beyond each of the eleven stories.

In compiling this volume I should like to thank the many pupils at Pimlico School who have read, listened and responded – as honestly as always – to these stories.

R. B.

Equal Rights

Bernard Ashley

'Can't you read?'

The man was looking at me and reaching under the counter as if he was going for his gun. He came up with another one of his signs to spread over the front of a paper.

'"Only two children at a time allowed in this shop"', he read out, loudly.

I looked across at the two kids in the corner. They were pretending to pick Penny Chews while they gawped at the girls on the magazines. O.K., I made three, but I wasn't there for the same reason as them. Couldn't he recognise business when he saw it?

'I'm not buying,' I said, 'I've come about the job.'

He frowned at me, in between watching the boys in the corner. 'What job?' he said. He was all on edge with three of us in the shop.

'"Reliable paper boy wanted"', I told him. '"Enquire within." It's in the window. I'm enquiring within.'

'Hurry up, you two!' he shouted. And then he frowned at me again as if I was something from outer space.

'But you're not a boy,' he said. '"Reliable paper *boy* required", that says. If I'd meant "boy *or girl*" I'd have put it on, wouldn't I? Or "paper *person*"!' He did this false laugh for the benefit of a man with a briefcase standing at the counter.

'Oh,' I said, disappointed. 'Only I'm *reliable*, that's all. I get up early with my dad, I'm never off school, and I can tell the difference between the *Sun* and the *Beano*.'

'I'm glad someone can,' the man with the briefcase said.

1

But the paper man didn't laugh. He was looking at me, hard.

'Where d'you live?' he asked.

'Round the corner.'

'Could you start at seven?'

'Six, if you like.'

'Rain or shine, winter and summer?'

'No problem.' I stared at him, and he stared at me. He looked as if he was deciding whether or not to give women the vote.

'All right,' he said, 'I'll give you a chance. Start Monday. Seven o'clock, do your own marking-up. Four pounds a week, plus Christmas tips. Two weeks' holiday without pay ...'

Now that he'd made up his mind he smiled at me over-doing the big favour.

'Is that what the boys get?' I asked. 'Four pounds a week?'

He started unwrapping a packet of fags. 'I don't see how that concerns you. The money suits or it doesn't. Four pounds is what I said, and four pounds is what I meant. Take it or leave it.' He looked at Briefcase again, shaking his head at the cheek of the girl.

I walked back to the door. 'I'll leave it, then,' I said, 'seeing the boys get five pounds, *and* a week's holiday with pay.' I knew all this because Jason used to do it. 'Thanks anyway, I'll tell my dad what you said ...'

'Please yourself.'

I slammed out of the shop. I was mad, I can tell you. Cheap labour, he was after: thought he was on to a good thing for a minute, you could tell that.

The trouble was, I really needed a bit of money coming in, saving for those shoes and things I wanted. There was no way I'd get them otherwise. But I wasn't going to be treated any different from the boys. I wouldn't have a shorter round or lighter papers, would I? Everything'd be the same, except the money.

2

I walked the long way home, thinking. It was nowhere near Guy Fawkes, and Carol Singing was even further away. So that really only left car washing – and they leave the rain to wash the cars round our way.

Hearing this baby cry gave me the idea. Without thinking about it I knocked at the door where the bawling was coming from.

The lady opened it and stared at me like you stare at double-glazing salesmen, when you're cross for being brought to the door.

' "Baby-play calling" ', I said – making up the name from somewhere.

The lady said, 'Eh?' and she looked behind me to see who was pulling my strings.

' "Baby-play" ', I said. 'We come and play with your baby in your own home. Keep it happy. Or walk it out – not going across main roads.'

She opened the door a bit wider. The baby crying got louder.

'How much?' she asked.

That really surprised me. I'd felt sorry about calling from the first lift of the knocker, and here she was taking me seriously.

'I don't know,' I said. 'Whatever you think . . .'

'Well . . .' She looked at me to see if she'd seen me before; to see if I was local enough to be trusted. Then I was glad I had the school jumper on, so she knew I could be traced. 'You push Bobby down the shops and get Mr Dawson's magazines, and I'll give you twenty pence. Take your time, mind . . .'

'All right,' I said. 'Thank you very much.'

She got this little push-chair out, and the baby came as good as gold – put its foot in the wheel a couple of times and nearly twisted its head off trying to see who I was, but I kept up the talking, and I stopped while it stared out a cat, so there wasn't any fuss.

When I got to the paper shop I took Bobby in with me.

3

'Afternoon,' I said, trying not to make too much of coming back. 'We've come down for Mr Dawson's papers, haven't we, Bobby?'

You should have seen the man's face.

'Mr Dawson's?' he asked, burning his finger on a match.

'Number twenty-nine?'

'Yes, please.'

'Are you . . .?' He nodded at Bobby and then at me as if he was making some link between us.

'That's right,' I said.

He fumbled at a pile behind him and lifted out the magazines. He laid them on the counter.

'Dawson', it said on the top. I looked at the titles to see what Mr Dawson enjoyed reading.

Workers' Rights was one of them. And *Trade Union Times* was the other. They had pictures on their fronts. One had two men pulling together on a rope. The other had a woman bus-driver waving out of her little window. They told you the sort of man Mr Dawson was – one of those trade union people you get on television kicking up a fuss over wages, or getting cross when women are treated different to men. Just the sort of bloke I could do with on my side, I thought.

The man was still fiddling about with his pile of magazines.

'Oh, look,' he said, with a green grin. 'I've got last month's *Pop Today* left over. You can have it if you like, with my compliments . . .'

'Thanks a lot,' I said. Now I saw the link in his mind. He thought I was Mr Dawson's daughter. He thought there'd be all sorts of trouble now, over me being offered lower wages than the boys.

'And about that job. Stupid of me, I'd got it wrong. What did I say – *four* pounds a week?'

'I think so,' I said. 'It sounded like a four.'

'How daft can you get? It was those kids in the corner. Took my attention off. Of course it's *five*, you realise that.

4

Have you spoken to your dad yet?'

'No, not yet.'

He stopped leaning so hard on the counter. 'Are you still interested?'

'Yes. Thank you very much.'

He came round the front and shook hands with me. 'Monday at seven,' he said. 'Don't be late . . .' But you could tell he was only saying it, pretending to be the big boss.

'Right.' I turned the push-chair round. 'Say ta-ta to the man, Bobby,' I said.

Bobby just stared, like at the cat.

The paper man leaned over. 'Dear little chap,' he said.

'Yeah, smashing. But Bobby's a girl, not a chap, aren't you, Bobby? At least, that's what Mrs Dawson just told me.'

I went out of the shop, while my new boss made this funny gurgling sound, and knocked a pile of papers on the floor.

He'd made a show-up of himself, found out too late that I wasn't Mr Dawson's daughter.

I ran and laughed and zig-zagged Bobby along the pavement. 'Good for us! Equal rights, eh, Bobby? Equal rights!'

But Bobby's mind was all on the ride. She couldn't care less what I was shouting. All she wanted was someone to push her fast, to feel the wind on her face. Boy or girl, it was all the same to her.

Swollen-Foot

Kenneth McLeish

King Laius of Thebes and his wife Jocasta were expecting a baby. But, before he was born, the god Apollo sent them a terrible warning.

'When your son grows up,' said the god, 'he will murder his father and marry his own mother.'

Laius and Jocasta were horrified. What could they do? How could they escape their fate? They made plans, quickly and secretly.

Jocasta's son was born, and when he was only one day old, the king gave him to one of the palace servants.

'Take him into the mountains,' he said. 'Leave him there to die. Fasten a nail through his ankles, so that no-one will want him. The birds and wild beasts will do the rest.'

The servant took the baby away. Sadly, he drove a long nail through the child's ankles, pinning them together. Then he went up the stony path to the high mountain pastures.

As he went, carrying the screaming baby, the man began to think.

'Poor little child! How can *he* hurt anyone? I can't leave him on this mountain for the birds and the wild beasts to eat. I'll give him to a shepherd, and ask him to take him far away from Thebes.'

On a mountain-top, he found a shepherd from Corinth, a place many miles from Thebes.

'My friend,' he said, 'please take this baby home. Take him away from Thebes. If he stays here, he must be killed.'

6

The shepherd from Corinth looked at the baby, and his heart filled with pity. Carefully, he drew the nail from the baby's ankles. He put cool ointment on the wound.

'Poor little child,' he said. 'I'll take you home, and keep you safe. And I'll call you Oedipus, because that means Swollen-foot.'

The two men each went home.

The Theban servant went back to King Laius.

'Your orders have been carried out,' he said. 'I left the baby on the mountain-side.'

Laius and Jocasta were overjoyed. Now the god's warning would never come true. The baby would never grow up. He would never murder his father, or marry his own mother.

The Corinthian shepherd took the baby Oedipus back to Corinth. He showed him to his master, King Polybos.

'What a beautiful child!' said the king. 'Let me have him to bring him up as my own son.'

The shepherd had six children of his own. Another baby would cost money to keep. Gladly, he agreed to do as the king asked. So, King Polybos and his queen took the baby, and brought him up as their own son. He was a prince of Corinth, and everyone respected him. But he kept the name Oedipus, so that everyone would know what had happened when he was a baby.

When Oedipus was eighteen, King Polybos and the queen gave a party in his honour. Everyone ate and drank, danced and sang, for days on end. Among the crowds was a visitor from Thebes. One night he got drunk, and began laughing at the young prince, and mocking him.

'Oedipus!' he said. 'Swollen-foot! What a name! Nobody knows where you got it from. Nobody even knows where you came from. Only one thing is certain – you aren't really a prince of Corinth. You aren't really the son of Polybos and his queen.'

Oedipus didn't know what to answer. He went to the king and queen and asked them for the truth.

'The man was quite right,' they said, sadly. 'No-one knows who you really are, or where you came from. Only the gods can tell you that.'

'All right,' said Oedipus. 'I'll go to Delphi, and ask Apollo.'

He set out, and travelled all the way to Delphi. But Apollo didn't answer his questions. Instead, he gave him a terrible warning.

'Oedipus,' he said, 'Oedipus, Swollen-foot! You must never go home again. For you are doomed to murder your father and marry your own mother!'

Oedipus was terrified.

'I must hide,' he thought. 'I must never go back to Corinth. How can I murder Polybos, or marry my own mother? I'll run away to a distant country, where no-one has ever seen or heard of me.'

He hurried away from Delphi, following the road inland. One day, he came to a crossroads. On the road, in front of him, there was a chariot drawn by two horses. There were six soldiers riding beside it, and in it was an old man, wearing a crown of laurel leaves.

'You! Stranger!' the old man shouted. 'Stand aside, and let us pass!'

'I won't,' said Oedipus. 'I've as much right on the road as you.'

The old man reached out, and slashed Oedipus across the face with his whip. Oedipus was furious. He drew his sword, and before the soldiers realised what was happening, he attacked them all, killing five of them and the old man, their master. Only one man escaped, and ran back down the road, screaming with terror.

Oedipus went on his way. Soon, he came to a city. Inside there was weeping and wailing. Everyone was frightened.

'What is it?' asked Oedipus. 'What's the matter?'

'Out there – out there, on the plain, there's a fearful monster. It has a woman's face and a lion's body. Every day it asks us the same riddle, and because we can't answer, every day it takes a young girl from the city and eats her alive.'

'What is the riddle?'

'This is what the monster says: "In the morning, I walk on four legs. At noon, I walk on two. In the evening, I walk on three. I walk on the earth, and across the sea. What am I?" That's the riddle and no one can answer it.'

Oedipus thought for a while.

'I think I can answer,' he said.

He walked out on the plain, and faced the monster.

'You! Monster!' he shouted. 'I've heard your riddle, and I know the answer.'

'You?' said the monster. 'Who are you?'

'I'm Oedipus, and your riddle does not trouble me! Here is your answer. In the morning of life, I walk on four legs – crawling like a baby. At noon, I walk upright on two legs – like a grown man. In the evening of life, I walk with a stick to help me – on three legs. I walk on earth and sail on the sea. The answer to your riddle is Mankind. You are talking about people, human beings, people like me.'

The monster gave a hiss of rage.

'You've guessed the riddle! But you'll suffer for it! You may be Oedipus, and know this answer, but there will be other questions for you one day. Will you know those answers, too?'

The monster vanished in a cloud of smoke. When they saw it was gone, all the townspeople came running out. They took Oedipus into the city in triumph.

'Sir,' they said, 'our queen is in mourning. Word has just come that our king is dead. But, she will see you, for you are Oedipus, and knew the answer.'

Oedipus went to see the queen.

'My lord,' she said, 'you guessed the riddle and saved the city. No city can survive without a king to protect it. Will you marry me and be our king?'

'Certainly,' said Oedipus. 'I'm a wanderer, with no home of my own. What's the name of your city?'

'This is the city of Thebes,' said Queen Jocasta.

So, Oedipus married Jocasta, and became King of Thebes. He ruled happily and well for several years. Four children were born to him and Jocasta, two boys and two girls. The city was happy and prosperous.[1] Everyone blessed the day when Oedipus came their way.

All except for one man. He went to the queen and begged her to send him away, far into the mountains, where no-one would ever find him.

'If that's what you want,' said Jocasta, 'of course you can go. You're a good servant. You helped the old king many years ago with that unwanted baby, and you were the one who brought back the news of the old king's death. Go into the mountains, and be happy.'

The servant went away. He knew the truth. He thought that by hiding he could stop anyone else from finding out. But the gods knew the truth as well.

Apollo was waiting for the right moment. When it came, the god sent a plague to torment Thebes. Cattle died, grass withered, babies were born dead. Nothing grew, and everything was barren and withered.

'The gods are angry,' said the priests. 'We must ask King Oedipus to help us, as he did when the riddling monster was here. He knew the answer then; perhaps he knows it now.'

They begged Oedipus to help them.

He sent a messenger to Delphi, to ask Apollo what to do. Four days went by, and there was still no news. On the fifth day, the messenger came back, galloping hard on a sweating horse.

'My lord,' he gasped, 'the god says this. The murderer of Laius, the old king, is here in the city. He is causing the plague, and we must find him and throw him out. That way the plague will end.'

'I'll find him. I'll find the murderer, and throw him out,'

1 rich

10

said Oedipus. 'I am Oedipus who knows the answers. I'll find the man and banish him.'

The search went on for days. Witnesses were found and questioned. No-one knew the truth. Jocasta began to laugh.

'Oracles!' she said. 'Gods! What do they know? They said Laius would be killed by his own son, many years ago. And, he wasn't. He was killed by a stranger, at a lonely crossroads, just before you came to Thebes.'

'A crossroads?' said Oedipus, startled. 'Killed at a crossroads? What did he look like, the old king?'

'He was tall. His hair was just beginning to turn grey. He looked very like you, Oedipus. In fact, he looked so like you, he might have been your father.'

Suddenly, Jocasta stopped, and looked hard at Oedipus.

'That servant!' she said. 'That old man we sent into the hills. He knows! He knows the truth!'

'Then, send for him,' snapped Oedipus. 'I must find out the truth, and clear this plague from the city.'

But now Jocasta, too, realised the truth.

'No, no, my lord,' she cried. 'Leave him where he is! Don't send for him!'

'Of course I'll send for him,' said Oedipus, angrily. 'I'm Oedipus and I must know the answer. Slaves! Go and fetch the man.'

The slaves rode off to the mountains to find the old servant. And Jocasta hid in the palace, knowing what he would say.

At last, the slaves returned. The old man was with them. He looked at Oedipus in terror.

'Speak!' said the king. 'You know who murdered Laius. Who was it? Speak now, and end the plague.'

'My lord, I can't,' said the old man. 'The gods ...'

'The gods?' interrupted Oedipus. 'It's me you should be afraid of, not the gods. Speak now, or I'll torture you until you tell the truth.'

'My lord,' said the old man, slowly. 'The murderer of

Laius, the old king, is the new King of Thebes. *You* are the man.'

Oedipus went pale. He remembered the crossroads, the old man he had killed, the soldiers, and the one who ran away. He remembered his promise to find Laius's murderer and banish him for ever. He felt sick. The man he had cursed was himself.

'Is that all?' he said. 'Is there nothing else you have to tell us?'

'My lord, I . . .'

'Tell us everything! Hide nothing! I am Oedipus, and I must know the answer – the whole answer, whatever it costs.'

'My lord, many years ago . . . a little baby . . . I took him into the mountains to kill him. But I couldn't do it . . . I hadn't the heart. I gave him to a shepherd from Corinth to take home. The poor little child . . . his ankles were nailed together. I hadn't the heart to leave him there to die.'

Oedipus broke in with a cry of agony. So that was the truth. Now he knew the answer! He knew who he was. He knew that the god's warning had come true. He had killed his father, and married his own mother. There were no more questions left. He was Oedipus, Swollen-foot, and he knew all the answers now.

Blindly, he ran into the palace to find Jocasta. Her door was locked. He kicked and hammered on it. At last, he broke his way in. There she was, his mother-wife, hanging dead in the middle of the room.

Oedipus cut her down. There was a gold pin fastening her dress at the shoulder. The servants watched in a silent group, to see what he would do.

Slowly, Oedipus took the pin from Jocasta's dress. Then, suddenly, he began jabbing it into his own eyes, time after time. Streams of blood ran down his cheeks, into his beard. No-one tried to stop him.

At last, Oedipus, now blind, staggered out of the palace into the sunlight.

'Apollo, god of the sun!' he shouted. 'You gave a warning, and it has come true. I've killed my father, and married my own mother. My sons and daughters are my brothers and sisters, too! I swore to banish Laius's murderer, so now I must drive myself into exile. Are you satisfied, Apollo? I am Oedipus, Swollen-foot, father-murderer, mother-husband. Now I know the answer! Nothing is hidden from me now.'

The people backed away from him in terror. Alone, blind, leaning on a stick, Oedipus stumbled out of Thebes. Now he knew the answer. When the gods send a warning, no man can prove them wrong.

The Holiday

George Layton

It wasn't fair. Tony and Barry were going. In fact, nearly all of them in Class Three and Four were going, except me. It wasn't fair. Why wouldn't my mum let me go?

'I've told you. You're not going camping. You're far too young.'

Huh! She said that last year.

'You said that last year!'

'You can go next year when you're a bit older.'

She'd said that last year, too.

'You said that last year an' all.'

'Do you want a clout?'

'Well you did, Mum, didn't you?'

'Go and wash your hands for tea.'

'Aw, Mum, everybody else is going to school camp. Why can't I?'

Because you're coming to Bridlington with me and your Auntie Doreen like you do every year.

'Because you're coming to Bridlington with me and your Auntie Doreen like you do every year!'

I told you. Oh, every year the same thing; my mum, me, and my Auntie Doreen at Mrs Sharkey's boarding house. I suppose we'll have that room next door to the lavatory: a double bed for my mum and my Auntie Doreen, and me on a camp bed behind a screen.

'I suppose we'll have that rotten room again.'

'Don't be cheeky! Mrs Sharkey saves that room for me

14

every year – last week in July and first week in August. It's
the best room in the house, facing the sea like that, and nice
and handy for the toilets. You know how important that is
for your Auntie Doreen.'

'Aw, Mum, I never get any sleep – the sea splashing on
one side and Auntie Doreen on the . . . aw!'

My mum gave me a great clout right across my head. She
just caught my ear an' all.

'Aw, bloomin' heck. What was that for?'

'You know very well. Now stop being so cheeky and go
and wash your hands.'

'Well, you've done it now. You've dislocated my jaw –
that's it now. I'll report you to that RSPCC thing, and
they'll sue you. You've really had it now . . . ow!'

She clouted me again, right in the same place.

'It's not fair. Tony's mum and dad are letting him go to
school camp, and Barry's. Why won't you let me go?'

She suddenly bent down and put her face right next to
mine, right close. She made me jump. Blimey, that moustache was getting longer. I wish she'd do something about
it—it's embarrassing to have a mum with a moustache.

'Now, listen to me, my lad. What Tony's mum and dad
do, and what Barry's mum and dad do, is their lookout.
You will come with me and your Auntie Doreen to
Bridlington and enjoy yourself like you do every year!'

Huh! Enjoy myself – that's a laugh for a start. How can
you enjoy yourself walking round Bridlington town centre
all day looking at shops? You can do that at home. Or else it
was bingo. 'Key-of-the-door, old-age pension, legs-eleven,
clickety-click' and all that rubbish. You could do that at
home as well. And when we did get to the beach, I had to
spend all day rubbing that oily sun stuff on my Auntie
Doreen's back. It was horrible. Then the rain would come
down and it was back to bingo. Honest, what's the point of
going on holiday if you do everything that you can do at
home? You want to do something different. Now camping,
that's different. Tony's dad had bought him a special

15

sleeping bag, just for going camping. Huh! I wish I had a dad.

'I bet if I had a dad, he'd let me go to school camp.'

I thought Mum was going to get her mad up when I said that, but she didn't at all.

'Go and wash your hands for tea, love. Your spam fritters will be ready in a minute.'

Ugh. Bloomin' spam fritters! Not worth washing your hands for!

'Yeh. All right.'

I started to go upstairs. Ooh, I was in a right mess now. I'd told all the other lads I was going. Our names had to be in by tomorrow. We had to give Mr Garnett our pound deposit. Well, I was going to go. I didn't care what Mum said, I was going to go – somehow! When I got to the top of the stairs, I kicked a tin wastepaper bin on the landing. It fell right downstairs. It didn't half make a clatter.

'What on earth are you doing?'

She would have to hear, wouldn't she?

'Eh. It's all right, Mum. I just tripped over the waste-paper bin. It's all right.'

'Oh, stop playing the goat and come downstairs. Your tea's ready.'

What was she talking about, playing the goat? I couldn't help tripping over a wastepaper bin. Well, I couldn't have helped it if I had tripped over it, an' well, I might have done for all she knew. Well, I wasn't going to wash my hands just for spam fritters. Oh, bet we have macaroni cheese as well. I went straight downstairs.

'Are your hands clean?'

'Yeh.'

'Here we are then. I've made some macaroni cheese as well.'

'Lovely.'

'C'mon. Eat it up quickly, then we'll have a nice bit of telly.'

I didn't say anything else about the school camp that

night. I knew it was no good. But I was going to go. I'd told Tony and Barry I was going, I'd told all the lads I was going. Somehow, I'd get my own way. When I got to school next morning, I saw Tony and Barry with Norbert Lightowler over by the Black Hole. That's a tiny snicket,[1] only open at one end, where we shove all the new lads on the first day of term. There's room for about twenty kids. We usually get about a hundred in. It's supposed to be good fun, but the new kids don't enjoy it very much. They get to enjoy it the next year.

'Hello, Tony. Hello, Barry.'

Norbert Lightowler spat out some chewing-gum. It just missed me.

'Oh, don't say "hello" to me then, will ya?'

'No. And watch where you're spitting your rotten chewing-gum – or you'll get thumped.'

Barry asked us all if we'd brought our pound deposit for school camp. Tony and Norbert had got theirs, of course. Nobody was stopping them going. I made out I'd forgotten mine.

'Oh heck. I must have left mine on the kitchen table.'

'Oh. I see. Well, maybe Garnett'll let you bring it tomorrow.'

I didn't say anything, but Norbert did.

'Oh, no. He said yesterday today's the last day. He said anybody not bringing their deposit today wouldn't be able to go. He did, you know.'

'Aw, shurrup, or I'll do you.'

'I'm only telling you.'

'Well, don't bother.'

Tony asked me if I'd learnt that poem for Miss Taylor. I didn't know what he was talking about.

'What poem?'

Norbert knew, of course. He brought a book out of his pocket.

1 passageway

'*Drake's Drum*. Haven't you learnt it?'

Oh crikey! *Drake's Drum*. With all this worry about trying to get to school camp. I'd forgotten all about it. Miss Taylor had told us to learn it for this morning.

'We're supposed to know it this morning, you know.'

'I know, Norbert, I know.'

Honest, Norbert just loved to see you in a mess, I suppose because he's usually in trouble himself.

'*I* know it. I spent all last night learning it. Listen:

'"'Drake he's in his hammock an' a
        thousand mile away.

Captain, art thou sleeping there below?

Slung a'tween the round shot in
        Nombres Dios bay ... "'

I snatched the book out of his hands.

'Come 'ere. Let's have a look at it.'

'You'll never learn it in time. Bell'll be going in a minute.'

'You were reading it, anyway.'

'I was not. It took me all last night to learn that.'

Barry laughed at him.

'What, all last night to learn three lines?'

'No, clever clogs. I mean the whole poem.'

Just then, the bell started going for assembly. Norbert snatched his book back.

'C'mon, we'd better get into line. Garnett's on playground duty.'

Norbert went over to where our class was lining up. Barry's in Class Four, so he went over to their column.

'See you at playtime.'

'Yeh. Tarah.'

While we were lining up, we were all talking. Mr Garnett just stood there with his hands on his hips, staring at us, waiting for us to stop.

'Thank you.'

Some of us heard his voice and stopped talking. Those that didn't carried on.

18

'Thank you.'

A few more stopped, and then a few more, till the only voice you could hear was Norbert Lightowler's, and as soon as he realized nobody else was talking, he shut up quickly.

'Thank you. If I have to wait as long as that for silence at the end of this morning's break, then we shall spend the whole break this afternoon learning how to file up in silence. Do you understand?'

We all just stood there, hardly daring to breathe.

'Am I talking to myself? Do you understand?'

Everybody mumbled 'Yes, sir', except Norbert Lightowler. He had to turn round and start talking to me and Tony.

'Huh! If he thinks I'm going to spend my playtime filing up in silence, he's got another think coming.'

'Lightowler!'

Norbert nearly jumped out of his skin.

'Are you talking to those boys behind you?'

'No, sir. I was just telling 'em summat . . .'

'Really?'

'Yes, sir . . . er . . . I was just . . . er . . . telling them that we have to give our pound in today, sir, for school camp, sir.'

'I want a hundred lines by tomorrow morning: "I must not talk whilst waiting to go into assembly."'

'Aw, sir.'

'Two hundred.'

He nearly did it again, but stopped just in time, or he'd have got three hundred.

'Right. When I give the word, I want you to go quietly into assembly. And no talking. Right – wait for it. Walk!'

Everybody walked in not daring to say a word. When we got into the main hall, I asked Tony for the book with *Drake's Drum* in, and during assembly, I tried to snatch a look at the poem but, of course, it was a waste of time. Anyway, I was more worried about my pound deposit for

Mr Garnett. After prayers, the Headmaster made an announcement about it.

'This concerns only the boys in Classes Three and Four. Today is the final day for handing in your school camp deposits. Those of you not in Three B must see Mr Garnett during morning break. Those of you in Three B will be able to hand in your money when Mr Garnett takes you after Miss Taylor's class. Right, School turn to the right. From the front, dismiss! No talking.'

I had another look at the poem while we were waiting for our turn to go.

' "Drake he's in his hammock an' a
    thousand mile away.
Captain, art thou sleeping there
    below?" '

Well, I knew the first two lines. Tony wasn't too bothered. He probably knew it.

'Don't worry. She can't ask everybody to recite it. Most likely she'll ask one of the girls. Anyway, what are you going to do about Garnett? Do you think he'll let you bring your pound deposit tomorrow?'

'Yeh, sure to.'

If only Tony knew that it'd be just as bad tomorrow. I had to get a pound from somewhere. Then I'd have about four weeks to get my mum to let me go. But I had to get my name down today or I'd ... I'd had it. Miss Taylor was already waiting for us when we got into our classroom.

'Come along, children. Settle down.'

Miss Taylor took us for English and Religious Instruction.

'Now you've all heard of the Ten Commandments . . .'

'Bloomin' hummer. What a let-off. Tony was grinning at me.

'Do you know the first of these Ten Commandments?'

Jennifer Greenwood put her hand up. She was top of the class every year. Everyone reckoned she was Miss Taylor's favourite.

'Yes, Jennifer.'

Jennifer Greenwood wriggled about a bit in her seat and went red. She's always going red.

'Please, Miss, it's English this morning, Miss; it's Religious Instruction tomorrow, Miss.'

Honest, I could've thumped her. Then Norbert put his hand up.

'Yes, Miss. You told us to learn *Drake's Drum* for this morning, Miss.'

I leaned across to Tony.

'I'll do him at playtime.'

'Quite right, Norbert. Thank you for reminding me. Now, who will recite it for me?'

Everybody shoved their hands up shouting, 'Miss, Miss, me Miss, Miss', so I thought I'd better look as keen as the rest of them.

'Miss! Miss! Miss!'

'I stretched my hand up high. I got a bit carried away. I was sure she'd pick one of the girls.

'Me, Miss. Please, Miss. Me, Miss!'

She only went and pointed at me. I couldn't believe it. 'Me, Miss?'

'Yes. You seem very keen for once. Stand up and speak clearly.'

I stood up as slowly as I could. My chair scraped on the floor and made a noise like chalk on the blackboard.

'Hurry up, and lift your chair up. Don't push it like that.'

Everybody was looking at me. Norbert, who sits in the front row, had turned round and was grinning.

'Er . . . um *Drake's Drum* . . . by Henry Newbolt . . .'

Miss Taylor lifted up her finger.

'*Sir* Henry Newbolt!'

'Yes, Miss.'

I was glad she stopped me. Anything to give me more time.

'Carry on.'

I took a deep breath. I could feel Norbert still grinning at me.

'Ahem. *Drake's Drum* . . . by Sir Henry Newbolt.'

I stopped: then I took another deep breath . . .

'"Drake is in his cabin and a thousand mile away . . ."'

I stopped again. I knew after the next line, I'd be in trouble.

'"Cap'n, art thou sleeping down below . . ."'

The whole class was listening. I didn't know what I was going to say next. I took another breath and I was just about to tell Miss Taylor I couldn't remember any more, when Norbert burst out laughing. Miss Taylor went over to him:

'What are you laughing at, Norbert?'

'Nothing, Miss.'

'You think you can do better – is that it?'

'No, Miss.'

'Stand up!'

Norbert stood up. Miss Taylor looked at me. 'Well done. That was a very dramatic opening. Sit down, and we'll see if Norbert Lightowler can do as well.'

I couldn't believe it. Tony could hardly keep his face straight.

Norbert went right through the poem. Miss Taylor had to help him once or twice, but he just about got through. Miss Taylor told him he hadn't done badly, but not quite as well as me. After that a few of the others recited it, and then we went on to do some English grammar.

After Miss Taylor, we had Mr Garnett. He gave the girls some arithmetic to do, while he sorted out the deposits for school camp. He went through the register, and everybody that was going gave him their pound deposit – until he got to me.

'I've forgotten it, sir.'

'You know today is the last day, don't you?'

'Yes, sir.'

'And all the names have to be in this morning? I told you all that yesterday, didn't I?'

22

'Yes, sir. Yes, sir – I'll bring my pound tomorrow, sir.'
Mr Garnett tapped his pencil.

'I'll put the pound in for you, and I want you to repay me
first thing tomorrow morning. All right?'

'Er . . . um . . . yes, sir. I think so, sir.'

'You do want to go to school camp?'

'Yes, sir.'

'Right then. Don't forget to give me your pound
tomorrow.'

'No, sir.'

I didn't know what I was going to do now. I reckoned the
best thing was to tell Mr Garnett the truth, so when the bell
went for playtime, I stayed behind in the classroom, and I
told him about my mum wanting me to go to Bridlington
with her and my Auntie Doreen. He told me not to worry,
and gave me a letter to give to my mum that night. I don't
know what it said, but after my mum had read it, she
put it in her pocket and said she'd give me a pound for
Mr Garnett in the morning.

'Can I go to camp, then?'

'Yes, if that's what you want.'

'I don't mind coming to Bridlington with you and Auntie
Doreen, if you'd rather . . .'

My mum just got hold of my face with both her hands.

'No, love, you go to school camp and enjoy yourself.'

So I did – go to school camp, that is – but I didn't enjoy
myself. It was horrible. They put me in a tent with Gordon
Barraclough: he's a right bully and he gets everybody on to
his side because they're all scared of him. I wanted to go in
Tony's and Barry's tent, but Mr Garnett said it would upset
all his schedules,[1] so I was stuck with Gordon Barraclough
and his gang. They made me sleep right next to the
opening, so when it rained, my sleeping-bag got soaked.
And they thought it was dead funny to pull my clothes out

1 plans

of my suitcase (my mum couldn't afford a rucksack) and throw them all over the place.

'Huh! Fancy going camping with a suitcase!'

'Mind your own business, Barraclough! My mum couldn't afford a proper rucksack. Anyway, I'm off to Bridlington on Sunday.'

And I meant it. Sunday was parents' visiting day, and my mum and Auntie Doreen were coming to see me on their way to Bridlington. So I was going to pack up all my stuff and go with them. Huh . . . I couldn't stand another week with Gordon Barraclough. I wished I'd never come.

So on Sunday morning, after breakfast in the big marquee, I packed everything into my suitcase and waited for my mum and my Auntie Doreen to come. They arrived at quarter to eleven.

'Hello, love. Well, isn't it grand here? You are having a nice time, aren't you?'

'Yeh, it's not bad, but I want to tell you summat.'

My mum wasn't listening. She was looking round the camp site.

'Well, it's all bigger than I thought. Is this your tent here?'

She poked her head through the flap. I could hear her talking to Gordon Barraclough and the others.

'No! No! No! Don't move, boys. Well, haven't you got a lot of room in here? It's quite deceiving from the outside.'

Her head came out again.

'Here, Doreen, you have a look in here. It's ever so roomy.'

She turned back to Gordon Barraclough.

'Well, bye-bye, boys. Enjoy the rest of your holiday. And thank you for keeping an eye on my little lad.'

I could hear them all laughing inside the tent. I felt sick.

'Mum, I want to ask you something.'

'In a minute, love, in a minute. Let's just see round the camp, and then we'll have a little natter before your Auntie Doreen and I go. Oh, and I want to say hello to Mr Garnett while I'm here. You know, on the way here today, I kept saying wouldn't it be lovely if I could take you on to Bridlington with us. Wasn't I, Doreen? But now I'm here, I can see you're all having a real good time together. You were right, love, it's much better to be with your friends than with two fuddy-duddies like us, eh, Doreen? Well, c'mon, love, aren't you going to show us round? We've got to get our bus for Bridlington soon.'

I showed them both round the camp site, and they went off just before dinner. I didn't feel like anything to eat myself. I just went to the tent and unpacked my suitcase.

Harold

Robert Leeson

Harold was a show off. Whatever you knew, he knew better. Whatever you had, he had better. And he could always win the argument by thumping you, because he was bigger. That was the main reason why we put up with him. Because the gang in the street round the corner from us would have slaughtered us if it hadn't been for Harold. With him around we could slog 'em any time. So, even when he gave you the pip, which was about ten times a day, you put up with him.

As I said, whatever was going new, his family had to have it first – sliced bread, gate-legged tables, copper fire irons, zip fasteners. They had rubber hot water bottles when the rest of us still had a hot brick in an old sock, a gas cooker when our Mams still cooked on the open range, an electric iron when Mam still heated her iron on the fire and spat on it to test the heat. They were first to have a five-shilling flip in a monoplane at Blackpool and they were first to have the telephone put in round our way. That was a dead loss because there was almost no one to ring up. It was sickening all round, the way they carried on. But worst of all was when they got the wireless.

Mr Marconi's invention was slow to arrive in Tarcroft. That is if you didn't count the crystal sets owned by the doctor and the man who hired out the charabanc.[1] Most people couldn't afford the wireless at first. But, of course,

1 coach

26

when Mr Marconi did arrive round our way, he came to Harold's house first.

We were sitting, the four of us, one day in the branches of the old oak tree that stands in the Meadows at the top of the Lane, when Harold spoke up:

'We're getting a wireless.'

There was silence for a second or two. What could you say? Then, just as Harold was going to speak again, Jammy said:

'So are we.'

'Get off. You're a little ligger,[1] Jammy.'

'Am not.'

'Are.'

'Want to bet?' asked Jammy, and he stretched himself out along his branch with hands behind his head, lying balanced. I don't know how he dared do it, twenty feet up.

'Want to bet?' he repeated.

Harold kept his mouth shut a minute, then burst out:

'All right, what make is it?'

'Cossor.'

'They're no good. Ours is a Phillips.'

'Get off. Cossor are better than Phillips any day.'

'Not.'

'Are.'

Bella made a face at me. Harold went on.

'Our wireless pole's twenty-five foot high.'

'Ours is thirty foot,' said Jammy.

'It never.'

' 'Tis 'n' all.'

'How d'you know?'

'Because our Dad climbed it when he fixed the aerial.'

Harold laughed like a drain.

'I always knew you were a monkey – that proves it.'

Jammy retorted: 'I bet your Dad couldn't climb the clothes post.'

1 liar

27

'My Dad wouldn't mess about climbing a wireless pole like a chimpanzee. We had a man in to fix ours. I bet your Dad didn't buy a wireless. Bet he put it together with bits and pieces.'

That was getting near the mark. Jammy's Dad was always fixing things.

'He never,' said Jammy, but he looked a bit funny.

'OK,' went on Harold. 'Bet you can't get Radio Luxemburg.'

'Can a duck swim? Course we can.'

'All right. What do you listen in to?'

'Ovaltineys.'

'They're no good. Joe the Sanpic Man's miles better.'

'Him? He's barmy, like you.'

'You're crackers.'

'You two give me a headache,' snapped Bella. But Harold wouldn't give up.

'How big's your wireless cabinet?' he asked craftily.

'How big's yours?' asked Jammy.

'Ya ha,' sneered Harold. 'You daren't say because ours is bigger and you know it.'

'Want to bet?' said Jammy. But I had a feeling he was getting desperate.

'OK. How much?' Harold was sure of himself and I began to feel sorry for Jammy.

'Ten to one.' Jammy was getting wild now.

'What in, conkers?'

'No, tanners.[1]'

'You never, that's a dollar[2] if you lose.'

Bella climbed down to a lower branch, hung on for a moment with her hands, then dropped to the ground.

'I'm off.'

I jumped down after her and Jammy followed. He was mad. Harold was laughing at him and I knew Jammy was

---

1 6d. = 2½p.
2 5s. = 25p.

making it up. Next day, though, we all went down to the Clough and played sliding in the old sandpit. It was smashing. I thought the stupid bet had been forgotten. I hated quarrels and so did Bella. But Harold hadn't forgotten at all.

Next week, Bella came round after school. That Wednesday there was to be a wedding in the Royal Family. School was closed for a half day. Would we like to come round and listen to it on their wireless? I thought to myself, Harold's Mam's as bad as he is.

When we got round there on the day, there was quite a crowd in their front room. Jammy's mother was there and some other women from our street and even one from round the corner.

She wore a funny big hat and had a put-on accent.

'Oh, I see you've had your sofa covered in rexine.'

'Oh, yes,' said Harold's Mam, 'it's the latest thing for *settees*.' She said the word 'settee' a bit louder, but the other woman didn't seem to notice.

'I'm not sure I fancy rexine, myself, it makes your drawers stick to your bottom.'

'Would you care for a cup of tea?' Harold's Mam said quickly to our Mam, who was staring out of the window to hide a smile.

While all this was going on, Harold was nudging Jammy and pointing to the corner. There on a special table stood the wireless, a big brown walnut cabinet with ornamental carving over the loudspeaker part and a line of polished buttons along the bottom. I thought Jammy looked sick. That wireless was enormous. It must have been two feet high and a foot across. Harold's mother switched on. There was a lot of crackling and spitting.

'Just atmospherics,' she said.

Jammy looked more cheerful. Perhaps it wouldn't work. But it did. Harold's mother gave the cabinet a very unladylike thump on the top and the crackling stopped. We could hear an organ playing and an old bloke droning on about something, then some singing, then a lot more crackling. Another hefty bang on the top and we heard a bloke with a posh voice telling us what we'd been listening to, in case we hadn't got it. I didn't think much to it all, but Mam and the other women said it was lovely. Then Jammy's mother piped up.

'On Saturday afternoon, I'd like you all round to our house for a cup of tea. There's a nice music programme we can listen in to.'

Harold's mother looked a bit peeved[1] but smiled and said: 'Delighted.' But Jammy looked green. Harold sniggered and whispered, 'That'll cost you a dollar.'

When we got outside I said: 'Hey, Harold, this bet's daft. Jammy hasn't got a dollar. It'll take him months to save that up.'

Bella nodded. But Harold smirked.

'Serve him right. He should keep his big mouth shut.' He turned round and swung on the gate. 'See you on Saturday, Jammy – have the money ready. I'll take two half dollars, or five bobs, ten tanners or twenty three-penny joeys. But not sixty pennies, 'cause it weighs your pockets down.'

Jammy slouched off down the road by himself.

Saturday tea time came round all too soon and there we were in Jammy's kitchen. They didn't have a front room. Jammy's mother had a good fire going, though it was the middle of July, and the kettle was boiling. The table was loaded with bread and butter, meat paste and corned beef sandwiches, and scones. We all sat down. Harold looked all round him, a fat grin on his face.

'Where's the wireless, Missis?'

'You speak when you're spoken to,' said his Mam.

'That's quite all right,' said Jammy's Mam. 'Alan, just take the dust cloth off will you, love.'

Jammy nipped sharply up from the table and whipped

1 annoyed

away a cloth that was hanging in the corner. I heard Harold choke on a mouthful of bread and butter. We all stared as Jammy switched on and the music came through with hardly any crackling.

But the cabinet! It must have been five foot high, not on a table, but standing on the floor. The loudspeaker part was decorated with cream-coloured scroll work. Below were two sets of knobs and switches, that seemed to go all the way down to the floor.

'Another butty,[1] Harold?' Jammy said sweetly. Bella and I sniggered. Mam tapped me on the head and said 'Sh!'

As soon as tea was over, Harold made an excuse and dashed out first. By the time we got to the door, he was heading off up the road.

'Whatever did our Harold dash off like that for?' asked his mother.

'Gone to dig up his money box, I should think,' chuckled Bella.

'I shall never understand what you have to giggle so much for, child. Come along,' said Bella's Mam, and swept away down the path, followed by Bella.

I turned to Jammy, who was his normal cheerful self.

'You won that one, Jammy,' I said. 'What are you going to do with that five bob?'

He grinned. 'Nowt. He can keep it. It was worth it just to see that look on his face. Besides,' he added and whispered in my ear, 'it wasn't a real wireless cabinet. It was an old second-hand kitchen cabinet Dad did up and fitted our wireless into the top part.'

'But what about all those knobs?'

'Oh, he put them on for show. He uses the bottom part to keep his beer in.'

I laughed all the way home.

Any time after that, when Jammy wanted to annoy Harold all he had to say was, 'Same to you – with knobs on!'

1 sandwich

Bella

Robert Leeson

Adam and Eve and Pinch-me-tight
Went down to the river to bathe.
Adam and Eve were drownded,
Who do you think was saved?
– Got you.

Bella was special. I thought so anyway, though I never let
on. She was Harold's sister, one year younger than him and
the same age as me. She had brown skin and very light
blonde hair, but deep brown eyes. Her parents christened
her Dorabella. They were always doing things like that. But
we called her Bella.

We were in the same class at school, but girls had to sit
on the other side of the room from boys, so I couldn't talk
to her then. And we had separate playgrounds. We didn't
meet on Sundays either, because their family went to a
posher chapel than ours. Sometimes in the evening, in
summer, though, when we were still in our Sunday best,
the whole family would go for a walk along the Meadow.
Then we'd all meet. Bella's Mam and Dad were on
speaking terms with ours, though our Dad was on the
Works and Bella's Dad was in business as a builder, and
fancied himself a bit.

We used to pass by, hot and tight in our clothes (Bella
used to have her hair pinned back till it pulled her eyebrows
up) and wishing we could have an ice cream or a drink of
pop. Our Dads would raise their hats and our Mams would

say, 'Good night, then.' Harold and I would shake our fists at one another and Bella would screw her nose up at me.

'What are you doing?' asked her mother.

'Got a fly on my nose,' answered Bella.

'Walk straight, girl,' said her Dad.

I'd sneak a look round and put my thumb to my nose at Harold, until I felt Dad's finger in my back.

'Stop acting the goat, lad.'

That was Sunday. It couldn't end too soon. But Saturday, that was different. On Saturday we all got together and no one watched what we were doing. Well, not much anyway.

Sometimes on hot summer days we'd go down to the Old River. The Old River was how it used to be, with rapids and a sluice, where the water tumbled down about twenty feet, foaming and boiling. The banks were all hung over with grass and weeds. The New River wasn't new any more. It was donkey's years since they cut the new channel and put locks in so that the flat boats could get up to the Works. It was deep, dirty and dangerous and if you went on the lock gates, the keeper might chase you off.

The Old River was deep, too, in places, but there were sandbanks where you could wade out. It was dirty, too, and in summer when the sun got on the water, it stank. Our parents told us off for going there, but we thought it was just the job.

The way down to the Old River was through the back lanes off the main road, past a little wood, keeping well clear of the houses at Tunnel Top, because their gang were too tough for us, and then full tilt down Gorse Hill. Gorse Hill was steep and green with short slippery turf and dotted all over were the gorse bushes with bright yellow blossoms. When the sun went down, the hill looked as though it were on fire. Right at the bottom was an old tow-path, broken here and there where the water had got in under the cinder track, and almost disappearing in bushes and weeds. We'd charge down Gorse Hill at full speed. The trick was to keep your legs going faster than your head so you didn't come a cropper – and then pull up short so you didn't run straight into the river.

We sat on the bank of the Old River one day, watching the boats pass through the locks across on the new cut.[1] It was so hot the sweat was running down my nose, even lying still.

'Tell you what,' said Jammy, jumping up. 'Let's go in the river.'

'Don't be dopey,' said Harold. 'We haven't got our cossies.'[2]

'I'm going in anyway,' said Jammy, peeling his shirt off.

'You're kidding.'

'Want to bet?' said Jammy, and ducked behind a bush. Next minute we heard a splash and he was in the water.

'Come on,' he yelled. 'It's smashing.' We looked round.

'Are you windy, or something?' shouted Jammy, kicking up his heels and spraying water all over the place. We didn't wait any longer. Harold and I picked a bush each and stripped down. Just then I heard a gasp from Harold. Bella was taking her frock off.

'Hey, Bella. You can't do that!'

'Get off. I want to come in as well,' she answered.

'You can't!'

'Why not?'

'Course you can't. Girls don't.'

'Ah, don't be mean, Harold. Let her come in if she wants to,' I said. 'Eh, Jammy?'

I looked round to Jammy for support, but he pretended he hadn't heard me.

'You stay on the bank and watch our clothes. We don't want kids from the locks pinching 'em,' said Harold.

So Bella stayed on the bank and looked glum while we went in the water. It was cool and smooth as milk, though

1 canal
2 swimming costumes

the sun was hot. I jumped from a sandbank and went right down. The water was green and I could see the sunlight showing through in a great yellow patch. I burst up again in the air and got a mouthful as Harold slapped the water with his arms. I slapped back. Jammy joined in. We made such a racket we didn't hear Bella shouting at first.

'Hey, come out. It's Constable Collins.'

'You're kidding.'

'Not. He's coming up from the locks.'

We panicked. Have you ever tried to run, when you're up to your waist in water? But we had no time to stop. If PC Collins told our parents, we were in real trouble. We charged off up the bank. Have you ever tried jumping gorse bushes when you're dressed in nothing but good intentions? In ten seconds flat we were half way up the hill and hiding behind some bushes.

Bella climbed up behind us more slowly.

'Where is he?' whispered Harold.

'You keep down. Your bum's showing,' said Bella. With my head pressed down in the grass I couldn't see her face, but I could tell from her voice she was enjoying this. We lay there trying to keep out of sight and clear of the gorse bushes at the same time. I could see Jammy wriggling about.

'What're you doing?'

'Trying to get my shorts on.'

'How did you get them?'

'Picked 'em up on the run.'

'Trust you, Jammy –' A few yards away, Harold raised his voice.

'You, Bella. Where are you?'

The bushes parted. Bella flopped down by my side. Without a word, she passed me my shorts and singlet.

'Did you get our clothes?' asked Harold from the other side of the bush. She smirked, and winked at me.

'Sorry, Harold. I was in such a rush I couldn't pick them all up.'

35

'What am I going to do?' yelled Harold.

'Hey, shut up. PC Collins'll hear you.'

'What am I going to do?'

'You'll have to wait till he's gone, won't you? Unless you want to borrow my nicks.'

'Don't be disgusting,' snarled Harold. He glared at her and crouched down behind a gorse bush. It was painful for him in more ways than one.

Next Saturday we gave the Old River a miss. But we went down there again before the summer was out. We had a swim now and then. And Bella came in with us. And Harold kept his mouth shut.

I'm keeping my mouth shut, too. PC Collins was nowhere near the Old River that day. Harold doesn't know that, and I'm not telling him.

How the Tortoise Became

Ted Hughes

When God made a creature, he first of all shaped it in clay. The he baked it in the ovens of the sun until it was hard. Then he took it out of the oven and, when it was cool, breathed life into it. Last of all, he pulled its skin on to it like a tight jersey.

All the animals got different skins. If it was a cold day, God would give to the animals he made on that day a dense, woolly skin. Snow was falling heavily when he made the sheep and the bears.

If it was a hot day, the new animals got a thin skin. On the day he made greyhounds and dachshunds and boys and girls, the weather was so hot God had to wear a sun hat and was calling endlessly for iced drinks.

Now on the day he made Torto, God was so hot the sweat was running down on to the tips of his fingers.

After baking Torto in the oven, God took him out to cool. Then he flopped back in his chair and ordered Elephant to fan him with its ears. He had made Elephant only a few days before and was very pleased with its big flapping ears. At last he thought that Torto must surely be cool.

'He's had as long as I usually give a little thing like him,' he said, and picking up Torto, he breathed life into him. As he did so, he found out his mistake.

Torto was not cool. Far from it. On that hot day, with no cooling breezes, Torto had remained scorching hot. Just as he was when he came out of the oven.

'Ow!' roared God. He dropped Torto and went hopping away on one leg to the other end of his workshop, shaking his burnt fingers.

'Ow, ow, ow!' he roared again, and plunged his hand into a dish of butter to cure the burns.

Torto meanwhile lay on the floor, just alive, groaning with the heat.

'Oh, I'm so hot!' he moaned. 'So hot! The heat. Oh, the heat!'

God was alarmed that he had given Torto life before he was properly cooled.

'Just a minute, Torto,' he said. 'I'll have a nice, thin, cooling skin on you in a jiffy. Then you'll feel better.'

But Torto wanted no skin. He was too hot as it was.

'No, no!' he cried. 'I shall stifle. Let me go without a skin for a few days. Let me cool off first.'

'That's impossible,' said God. 'All creatures must have skins.'

'No, no!' cried Torto, wiping the sweat from his little brow. 'No skin!'

'Yes!' cried God.

'No!' cried Torto.

'Yes!'

'No!'

God made a grab at Torto, who ducked and ran like lightning under a cupboard. Without any skin to cumber[1] his movements, Torto felt very light and agile.

'Come out!' roared God, and got down on his knees to grope under the cupboard for Torto.

In a flash, Torto was out from under the end of the cupboard, and while God was still struggling to his feet, he

1 limit

38

ran out through the door and into the world, without a skin.

The first thing he did was to go to a cool pond and plunge straight into it. There he lay, for several days, just cooling off. Then he came out and began to live among the other creatures. But he was still very hot. Whenever he felt his own heat getting too much for him, he retired to his pond to cool off in the water. In this way, he found life pleasant enough.

Except for one thing. The other creatures didn't approve of Torto.

They all had skins. When they saw Torto without a skin, they were horrified.

'But he has no skin!' cried Porcupine.

'It's disgusting!' cried Yak. 'It's indecent!'

'He's not normal. Leave him to himself,' said Sloth.

So all the animals began to ignore Torto. But they couldn't ignore him completely, because he was a wonderfully swift runner, and whenever they held a race, he won it. He was so nimble without a skin that none of the other creatures could hope to keep up with him.

'I'm a genius-runner,' he said. 'You should respect me. I am faster than the lot of you put together. I was made different.'

But the animals still ignored him. Even when they had to give him the prizes for winning all the races, they still ignored him.

'Torto is a very swift mover,' they said. 'And perhaps swifter than any of us. But what sort of a creature is he? No skin!'

And they all turned up their noses.

At first, Torto didn't care at all. When the animals collected together, with all their fur brushed and combed and set neatly, he strolled among them, smiling happily, naked.

'When will this disgusting creature learn to behave?' cried Turkey, loudly enough for everyone to hear.

'Just take no notice of him,' said Alligator, and lumbered round, in his heavy armour, to face in the opposite direction.

All the animals turned round to face in the opposite direction.

When Torto went up to Grizzly Bear to ask what everyone was looking at, Grizzly Bear pretended to have a fly in his ear. When he went to Armadillo, Armadillo gathered up all his sons and daughters and led them off without a word or a look.

'So that's your game, is it?' said Torto to himself. Then aloud, he said: 'Never mind. Wait till it comes to the races.'

When the races came, later in the afternoon, Torto won them all. But nobody cheered. He collected the prizes and went off to his pond alone.

'They're jealous of me,' he said. 'That's why they ignore me. But I'll punish them: I'll go on winning all the races.'

That night, God came to Torto and begged him to take a proper skin before it was too late. Torto shook his head:

'The other animals are snobs,' he said. 'Just because they are covered with a skin, they think everyone else should be covered with one too. That's snobbery. But I shall teach them not to be snobs by making them respect me. I shall go on winning all the races.'

And so he did. But still the animals didn't respect him. In fact, they grew to dislike him more and more.

One day there was a very important race-meeting, and all the animals collected at the usual place. But the minute Torto arrived they simply walked away. Simply got up and walked away. Torto sat on the race-track and stared after them. He felt really left out.

'Perhaps,' he thought sadly, 'it would be better if I had a skin. I mightn't be able to run then, but at least I would have friends. I have no friends. Besides, after all this practice, I would still be able to run quite fast.'

But as soon as he said that he felt angry with himself.

'No!' he cried. 'They are snobs. I shall go on winning their races in spite of them. I shall teach them a lesson.'

And he got up from where he was sitting and followed them. He found them all in one place, under a tree. And the races were being run.

'Hey!' he called as he came up to them. 'What about me?'

But at that moment, Tiger held up a sign in front of him. On the sign, Torto read: 'Creatures without skins are not allowed to enter.'

Torto went home and brooded. God came up to him.

'Well, Torto,' said God kindly, 'would you like a skin yet?'

Torto thought deeply.

'Yes,' he said at last, 'I would like a skin. But only a very special sort of skin.'

'And what sort of a skin is that?' asked God.

'I would like,' said Torto, 'a skin that I can put on, or take off, just whenever I please.'

God frowned.

'I'm afraid,' he said, 'I have none like that.'

'Then make one,' replied Torto. 'You're God.'

God went away and came back within an hour.

'Do you want a beautiful skin?' he asked. 'Or do you mind if it's very ugly?'

'I don't care what sort of a skin it is,' said Torto, 'so long as I can take it off and put it back on again just whenever I please.'

God went away again, and again came back within an hour.

'Here it is. That's the best I can do.'

'What's this!' cried Torto. 'But it's horrible!'

'Take it or leave it,' said God, and walked away.

Torto examined the skin. It was tough, rough, and stiff. 'It's like a coconut,' he said. 'With holes in it.'

And so it was. Only it was shiny. When he tried it on, he found it quite snug. It had only one disadvantage. He could move only very slowly in it.

41

'What's the hurry?' he said to himself then. 'When it comes to moving, who can move faster than me?'

And he laughed. Suddenly he felt delighted. Away he went to where the animals were still running their races.

As he came near to them, he began to think that perhaps his skin was a little rough and ready. But he checked himself:

'Why should I dress up for them?' he said. 'This rough old thing will do. The races are the important thing.'

Tiger lowered his notice and stared in dismay as Torto swaggered[1] past him. All the animals were now turning and staring, nudging each other, and turning, and staring.

'That's a change, anyway,' thought Torto.

Then, as usual, he entered for all the races.

The animals began to talk and laugh among themselves as they pictured Torto trying to run in his heavy new clumsy skin.

'He'll look silly, and then how we'll laugh.' And they all laughed.

But when he took his skin off at the starting-post, their laughs turned to frowns.

He won all the races, then climbed back into his skin to collect the prizes. He strutted in front of all the animals.

'Now it's my turn to be snobbish,' he said to himself.

Then he went home, took off his skin, and slept sweetly. Life was perfect for him.

This went on for many years. But though the animals would now speak to him, they remembered what he had been. That didn't worry Torto, however. He became very fond of his skin. He began to keep it on at night when he came home after the races. He began to do everything in it, except actually race. He crept around slowly, smiling at the leaves, letting the days pass.

There came a time when there were no races for several weeks. During all this time Torto never took his skin off

1 moved boastfully

once. Until, when the first race came round at last, he found he could not take his skin off at all, no matter how he pushed and pulled. He was stuck inside it. He strained and squeezed and gasped, but it was no use. He was stuck.

However, he had already entered for all the races, so he had to run.

He lined up, in his skin, at the start, alongside Hare, Greyhound, Cheetah and Ostrich. They were all great runners, but usually he could beat the lot of them easily. The crowd stood agog.[1]

'Perhaps,' Torto was thinking, 'my skin won't make much difference. I've never really tried to run my very fastest in it.'

The starter's pistol cracked, and away went Greyhound, Hare, Cheetah and Ostrich, neck and neck. Where was Torto?

The crowd roared with laughter.

Torto had fallen on his face and had not moved an inch. At his first step, cumbered by his stiff, heavy skin, he had fallen on his face. But he tried. He climbed back on to his feet and made one stride, slowly, then a second stride, and was just about to make a third when the race was over and Cheetah had won. Torto had moved not quite three paces. How the crowd laughed!

And so it was with all the races. In not one race did Torto manage to make more than three steps, before it was over.

The crowd was enjoying itself. Torto was weeping with shame.

After the last race, he turned to crawl home. He only wanted to hide. But though the other animals had let him go off alone when he had the prizes, now they came alongside him, in a laughing, mocking crowd.

'Who's the slowest of all the creatures?' they shouted. 'Torto is!'

'Who's the slowest of all the creatures?'

1 very curious

43

'Torto is!'
all the way home.

After that, Torto tried to keep himself out of sight, but the other animals never let him rest. Whenever any of them chanced to see him, they would shout at the tops of their voices:

'Who's the slowest of all the creatures?'

And every other creature within hearing would answer, at the tops of their voices:

'Torto is!'

And that is how Torto came to be known as 'Tortoise'.

In The Middle of The Night

Philippa Pearce

In the middle of the night a fly woke Charlie. At first he lay listening, half-asleep, while it swooped about the room. Sometimes it was far; sometimes it was near – that was what had woken him; and occasionally it was very near indeed. It was very, very near when the buzzing stopped: the fly had alighted on his face. He jerked his head up; the fly buzzed off. Now he was really awake.

The fly buzzed widely about the room, but it was thinking of Charlie all the time. It swooped nearer and nearer. Nearer . . .

Charlie pulled his head down under the bedclothes. All of him under the bedclothes, he was completely protected; but he could hear nothing except his heartbeats and his breathing. He was overwhelmed by the smell of warm bedding, warm pyjamas, warm himself. He was going to suffocate. So he rose suddenly up out of the bedclothes; and the fly was waiting for him. It dashed at him. He beat at it with his hands. At the same time he appealed to his younger brother, Wilson, in the next bed: 'Wilson, there's a fly!'

Wilson, unstirring, slept on.

Now Charlie and the fly were pitting their wits against each other: Charlie pouncing on the air where he thought the fly must be; the fly sliding under his guard towards his face. Again and again the fly reached Charlie; again and again, almost simultaneously,[1] Charlie dislodged him. Once he hit the fly – or, at least, hit where the fly had been a second before, on the side of his head; the blow was so hard that his head sang with it afterwards.

Then suddenly the fight was over; no more buzzing. His blows – or rather, one of them – must have told.

He laid his head back on the pillow, thinking of going to sleep again. But he was also thinking of the fly, and now he noticed a tickling in the ear he turned to the pillow.

It must be – it *was* – the fly.

He rose in such panic that the waking of Wilson really seemed to him a possible thing, and useful. He shook him repeatedly: 'Wilson – Wilson, I tell you, there's a fly in my ear!'

Wilson groaned, turned over very slowly like a seal in water, and slept on.

The tickling in Charlie's ear continued. He could just imagine the fly struggling in some passageway too narrow for its wing-span. He longed to put his finger into his ear and rattle it round, like a stick in a rabbit-hole; but he was afraid of driving the fly deeper into his ear.

Wilson slept on.

Charlie stood in the middle of the bedroom floor, quivering[2] and trying to think. He needed to see down his ear, or to get someone else to see down it. Wilson wouldn't do; perhaps Margaret would.

Margaret's room was next door. Charlie turned on the light as he entered: Margaret's bed was empty. He was startled, and then thought that she must have gone to the lavatory. But there was no light from there. He listened carefully: there was no sound from anywhere, except for the usual snuffling moans from the hall, where Floss slept and dreamt of dog-biscuits. The empty bed was mystifying;

1 at the same time
2 trembling

46

but Charlie had his ear to worry about. It sounded as if there were a pigeon inside it now.

Wilson asleep; Margaret vanished; that left Alison. But Alison was bossy, just because she was the eldest; and, anyway, she would probably only wake Mum. He might as well wake Mum himself.

Down the passage and through the door always left ajar. 'Mum,' he said. She woke, or at least half-woke, at once: 'Who is it? Who? Who? What's the matter? What? –'

'I've a fly in my ear.'

'You can't have.'

'It flew in.'

She switched on the bedside light, and, as she did so, Dad plunged beneath the bedclothes with an exclamation and lay still again.

Charlie knelt at his mother's side of the bed and she looked into his ear. 'There's nothing.'

'Something crackles.'

'It's wax in your ear.'

'It tickles.'

'There's no fly there. Go back to bed and stop imagining things.'

His father's arm came up from below the bedclothes. The hand waved about, settled on the bedside light and clicked it out. There was an upheaval of bedclothes and a comfortable grunt.

'Good night,' said Mum from the darkness. She was already allowing herself to sink back into sleep again.

'Good night,' Charlie said sadly. Then an idea occurred to him. He repeated his good night loudly and added some coughing, to cover the fact that he was closing the bedroom door behind him – the door that Mum kept open so that she could listen for her children. They had outgrown all that kind of attention, except possibly for Wilson. Charlie had shut the door against Mum's hearing because he intended to slip downstairs for a drink of water – well, for a drink and perhaps a snack. That fly-business had woken him up and also weakened him: he needed something.

He crept downstairs, trusting to Floss's good sense not to make a row. He turned the foot of the staircase towards the kitchen, and there had not been the faintest whimper from her, far less a bark. He was passing the dog-basket when he had the most unnerving sensation[1] of something being wrong there – something unusual, at least. He could not have said whether he had heard something or smelt something – he could certainly have seen nothing in the blackness: perhaps some extra sense warned him.

'Floss?' he whispered, and there was the usual little scrabble and snuffle. He held out his fingers low down for Floss to lick. As she did not do so at once, he moved them towards her, met some obstruction –

'Don't poke your fingers in my eyes!' a voice said, very low-toned and cross. Charlie's first, confused thought was that Floss had spoken: the voice was familiar – but then a voice from Floss should *not* be familiar; it should be strangely new to him –

He took an uncertain little step towards the voice, tripped over the obstruction, which was quite wrong in shape and size to be Floss, and sat down. Two things now happened. Floss, apparently having climbed over the obstruction, reached his lap and began to lick his face. At the same time a human hand fumbled over his face, among the slappings of Floss's tongue, and settled over his mouth. 'Don't make a row! Keep quiet!' said the same voice. Charlie's mind cleared: he knew, although without understanding, that he was sitting on the floor in the dark with Floss on his knee and Margaret beside him.

Her hand came off his mouth.

'What are you doing here, anyway, Charlie?'

'I like that! What about you? There was a fly in my ear.'

'Go on!'

1 feeling

48

'There was.'

'Why does that make you come downstairs?'

'I wanted a drink of water.'

'There's water in the bathroom.'

'Well, I'm a bit hungry.'

'If Mum catches you . . .'

'Look here,' Charlie said, 'you tell me what you're doing down here.'

Margaret sighed. 'Just sitting with Floss.'

'You can't come down and just sit with Floss in the middle of the night.'

'Yes, I can. I keep her company. Only at weekends, of course. No one seemed to realize what it was like for her when those puppies went. She just couldn't get to sleep for loneliness.'

'But the last puppy went weeks ago. You haven't been keeping Floss company every Saturday night since then.'

'Why not?'

Charlie gave up. 'I'm going to get my food and drink,' he said. He went into the kitchen, followed by Margaret, followed by Floss.

They all had a quick drink of water. Then Charlie and Margaret looked into the larder: the remains of a joint; a very large quantity of mashed potato; most of a loaf; eggs; butter; cheese . . .

'I suppose it'll have to be just bread and butter and a bit of cheese,' said Charlie. 'Else Mum might notice.'

'Something hot,' said Margaret. 'I'm cold from sitting in the hall comforting Floss. I need hot cocoa, I think.' She poured some milk into a saucepan and put it on the hot plate. Then she began a search for the tin of cocoa. Charlie, standing by the cooker, was already absorbed[1] in the making of a rough cheese sandwich.

The milk in the pan began to steam. Given time, it rose in the saucepan, peered over the top, and boiled over on to

1 very interested

49

the hot plate, where it sizzled loudly. Margaret rushed back and pulled the saucepan to one side. 'Well, really, Charlie! Now there's that awful smell! It'll still be here in the morning, too.'

'Set the fan going,' Charlie suggested.

The fan drew the smell from the cooker up and away through a pipe to the outside. It also made a loud roaring noise. Not loud enough to reach their parents, who slept on the other side of the house – that was all that Charlie and Margaret thought of.

Alison's bedroom, however, was immediately above the kitchen. Charlie was eating his bread and cheese, Margaret was drinking her cocoa, when the kitchen door opened and there stood Alison. Only Floss was pleased to see her.

'Well!' she said.

Charlie muttered something about a fly in his ear, but Margaret said nothing. Alison had caught them red-handed. She would call Mum downstairs, that was obvious. There would be an awful row.

Alison stood there. She liked commanding a situation.

Then, instead of taking a step backwards to call up the stairs to Mum, she took a step forward into the kitchen. 'What are you having, anyway?' she asked. She glanced with scorn at Charlie's poor piece of bread and cheese and at Margaret's cocoa. She moved over to the larder, flung open the door, and looked searchingly inside. In such a way must Napoleon have viewed a battlefield before victory.

Her gaze fell upon the bowl of mashed potato. 'I shall make potato-cakes,' said Alison.

They watched while she brought the mashed potato to the kitchen table. She switched on the oven, fetched her other ingredients, and began mixing.

'Mum'll notice if you take much of that potato,' said Margaret.

But Alison thought big. 'She may notice if some potato is missing,' she agreed. 'But if there's none at all, and if the bowl it was in is washed and dried and stacked away with the others, then she's going to think she must have made a mistake. There just can never have been any mashed potato.'

Alison rolled out her mixture and cut it into cakes; then she set the cakes on a baking-tin and put it in the oven.

Now she did the washing up. Throughout the time they were in the kitchen. Alison washed up and put away as she went along. She wanted no one's help. She was very methodical, and she did everything herself to be sure that nothing was left undone. In the morning there must be no trace left of the cooking in the middle of the night.

'And now,' said Alison, 'I think we should fetch Wilson.'

The other two were aghast[1] at the idea; but Alison was firm in her reasons. 'It's better if we're all in this together, Wilson as well. Then if the worst comes to the worst, it won't be just us three caught out, with Wilson hanging on to Mum's apron-strings, smiling innocence. We'll all be for it together; and Mum'll be softer with us if we've got Wilson.'

They saw that, at once. But Margaret still objected: 'Wilson will tell. He just always tells everything. He can't help it.'

Alison said, 'He always tells everything. Right: we'll give him something *to* tell, and then see if Mum believes him. We'll do an entertainment for him. Get an umbrella from the hall and Wilson's sou'wester[2] and a blanket or a rug or something. Go on.'

They would not obey Alison's orders until they had heard her plan; then they did. They fetched the umbrella and the hat, and lastly they fetched Wilson, still sound asleep, slung between them in his eiderdown. They propped him in a chair at the kitchen table, where he still slept.

By now the potato-cakes were done. Alison took them out of the oven and set them on the table before Wilson.

1 horrified
2 waterproof hat

She buttered them, handing them in turn to Charlie and Margaret and helping herself. One was set aside to cool for Floss.

The smell of fresh-cooked, buttery potato-cake woke Wilson, as was to be expected. First his nose sipped the air, then his eyes opened, his gaze settled on the potato-cakes.

'Like one?' Alison asked.

Wilson opened his mouth wide and Alison put a potato-cake inside, whole.

'They're paradise-cakes,' Alison said.

'Potato-cakes?' said Wilson, recognizing the taste.

'No, paradise-cakes, Wilson,' and then, stepping aside, she gave him a clear view of Charlie's and Margaret's entertainment, with the umbrella and the sou'wester hat and his eiderdown. 'Look, Wilson, look.'

Wilson watched with wide-open eyes, and into his wide-open mouth Alison put, one by one, the potato-cakes that were his share.

But, as they had foreseen, Wilson did not stay awake for very long. When there were no more potato-cakes, he yawned, drowsed, and suddenly was deeply asleep. Charlie and Margaret put him back into his eiderdown and took him upstairs to bed again. They came down to return the umbrella and the sou'wester to their proper places, and to see Floss back into her basket. Alison, last out of the kitchen, made sure that everything was in its place.

The next morning Mum was down first. On Sunday she always cooked a proper breakfast for anyone there in time. Dad was always there in time; but this morning Mum was still looking for a bowl of mashed potato when he appeared.

'I can't think where it's gone,' she said. 'I can't think.'

'I'll have the bacon and eggs without the potato,' said Dad; and he did. While he ate, Mum went back to searching.

Wilson came down, and was sent upstairs again to put on a dressing-gown. On his return he said that Charlie was still asleep and there was no sound from the girls' rooms either. He said he thought they were tired out. He went on talking while he ate his breakfast. Dad was reading the paper and Mum had gone back to poking about in the larder for the bowl of mashed potato, but Wilson liked talking even if no one would listen. When Mum came out of the larder for a moment, still without her potato, Wilson was saying: '. . . and Charlie sat in an umbrella-boat on an eiderdown-sea, and Margaret pretended to be a sea-serpent, and Alison gave us paradise-cakes to eat. Floss had one too, but it was too hot for her. What are paradise-cakes? Dad, what's a paradise-cake?'

'Don't know,' said Dad, reading.

'Mum, what's a paradise-cake?'

'Oh, Wilson, don't bother so when I'm looking for something . . . When did you eat this cake, anyway?'

'I told you. Charlie sat in his umbrella-boat on an eiderdown-sea and Margaret was a sea-serpent and Alison –'

'Wilson,' said his mother, 'you've been dreaming.'

'No, really – really!' Wilson cried.

But his mother paid no further attention. 'I give up,' she said. 'That mashed potato: it must have been last weekend . . .' She went out of the kitchen to call the others: 'Charlie! Margaret! Alison!'

Wilson, in the kitchen, said to his father, 'I wasn't dreaming. And Charlie said there was a fly in his ear.'

Dad had been quarter-listening; now he put down his paper. 'What?'

'Charlie had a fly in his ear.'

Dad stared at Wilson. 'And what did you say that Alison fed you with?'

'Paradise-cakes. She'd just made them, I think, in the middle of the night.'

'What were they like?'

'Lovely. Hot, with butter. Lovely.'

'But were they – well, could they have had any mashed potato in them, for instance?'

53

In the hall Mum was finishing her calling: 'Charlie! Margaret! Alison! I warn you now!'

'I don't know about that,' Wilson said. 'They were paradise-cakes. They tasted a bit like the potato-cakes Mum makes, but Alison said they weren't. She specially said they were paradise-cakes.'

Dad nodded. 'You've finished your breakfast. Go up and get dressed, and you can take this' – he took a coin from his pocket – 'straight off to the sweetshop. Go on.'

Mum met Wilson at the kitchen door: 'Where's he off to in such a hurry?'

'I gave him something to buy sweets with,' said Dad. 'I wanted a quiet breakfast. He talks too much.'

The Monkey's Paw

W. W. Jacobs

The night was cold and wet, but in the small parlour the
blinds were drawn and the fire burned brightly. Father and
son were playing chess. The white-haired old lady was
knitting placidly[1] by the fire.

'Listen to the wind,' said Mr White. 'I should hardly
think that he'd come tonight.'

Father and son sat with hands poised over the board.

'That's the worst of living so far out,' bawled Mr White,
with sudden violence; 'of all the beastly, slushly, out-of-
the-way places to live in, this is the worst.'

'Never mind, dear,' said his wife soothingly.

Mr White looked up sharply, and the words died away on
his lips.

'There he is,' said Herbert White, as the gate banged
loudly and heavy footsteps came toward the door.

The old man rose with haste and, opening the door, was
heard speaking with the new arrival. Mrs White coughed
gently as her husband entered the room, followed by a tall,
burly man.

'Sergeant-Major Morris,' he said, introducing him.

The sergeant-major shook hands and, taking the seat by
the fire, watched contentedly while his host got out whisky
and tumblers.

At the third glass his eyes got brighter, and he began to
talk. The little family circle regarded with eager interest

1 calmly

55

this visitor from distant parts who spoke of wild scenes and valiant[1] deeds of wars and plagues, and strange peoples.

'Twenty-one years of it,' said Mr White, nodding at his wife and son. 'When he went away he was a slip of a youth. Now look at him.'

'He don't look to have taken much harm,' said Mrs White politely.

'I'd like to go to India myself,' said the old man, 'just to look round a bit, you know.'

'Better where you are,' said the sergeant-major, shaking his head. He put down the empty glass and, sighing softly, shook it again.

'I should like to see those old temples,' said the old man. 'What was that you started telling me the other day about a monkey's paw or something, Morris?'

'Nothing,' said the soldier hastily. 'Leastways nothing worth hearing.'

'Monkey's paw?' said Mrs White curiously.

'Well, it's just a bit of what you might call magic, perhaps,' said the sergeant-major off-handedly.

His three listeners leaned forward eagerly. The visitor absent-mindedly put his empty glass to his lips and then set it down again. His host filled it for him.

'To look at,' said the sergeant-major, fumbling in his pocket, 'it's just an ordinary little paw, dried to a mummy.'

He took something out of his pocket. Mrs White drew back with a grimace,[2] but her son, taking it, examined it curiously.

'And what is there special about it?' inquired Mr White as he took it from his son and, having examined it, placed it upon the table.

'It had a spell put on it by an old fakir,' said the sergeant-major, 'a very holy man. He wanted to show that fate ruled people's lives and that those who interfered with

1 brave
2 ugly look

56

it did so to their sorrow. He put a spell on it so that three separate men could each have three wishes from it.'

'Well, why don't you have three, sir?' said Herbert White cleverly.

'I have,' he said quietly, and his blotchy face whitened.

'And did you really have the three wishes granted?' asked Mrs White.

'I did,' said the sergeant-major, and his glass tapped against his strong teeth.

'And has anybody else wished?' persisted the old lady.

'Yes. The first man had his three wishes. I don't know what the first two were, but the third was for death. That's how I got the paw.'

His tones were so grave that a hush fell upon the group.

'If you've had your three wishes, it's no good to you then, Morris,' said the old man at last. 'What do you keep it for?'

The soldier shook his head. 'Fancy, I suppose,' he said slowly. 'I did have some idea of selling it, but I don't think I will. It has caused enough mischief already. Besides, people won't buy. They think it's a fairy tale, some of them; and those who do think anything of it want to try it first and pay me afterwards.'

'If you could have another three wishes,' said the old man, eyeing him keenly, 'would you have them?'

'I don't know,' said the other. 'I don't know.'

He took the paw and, dangling it between his forefinger and thumb, suddenly threw it upon the fire. White, with a slight cry, stooped down and snatched it off.

'Better let it burn,' said the soldier solemnly.[1]

'If you don't want it, Morris,' said the other, 'give it to me.'

'I won't,' said his friend. 'I threw it on the fire. If you keep it, don't blame me for what happens. Pitch it on the fire again like a sensible man.'

1 seriously

The other shook his head and examined his new possession closely. 'How do you do it?' he asked.

'Hold it up in your right hand and wish aloud,' said the sergeant-major, 'but I warn you.'

'Sounds like the *Arabian Nights*,' said Mrs White, as she rose and began to set the supper. 'Don't you think you might wish for four pairs of hands for me?'

Her husband drew the paw from his pocket, and then all three burst into laughter as the sergeant-major, with a look of alarm on his face, caught him by the arm.

'If you must wish,' he said gruffly, 'wish for something sensible.'

Mr White dropped it back in his pocket and motioned his friend to the table. During supper the paw was partly forgotten, and afterwards the three sat listening to more of the soldier's adventures in India.

'If the tale about the monkey's paw is not more truthful than those he has been telling us,' said Herbert, as the door closed behind their guest, 'we shan't make much out of it.'

'Did you give him anything for it, father?' asked Mrs White looking at her husband closely.

'A trifle,'[1] he said. 'He didn't want it, but I made him take it. And he begged me again to throw it away.'

'Likely,' said Herbert, with pretended horror. 'Why, we're going to be rich and famous and happy. Wish to be an emperor, father, to begin with; then you can't be henpecked.'

Mr White took the paw from his pocket and eyed it doubtfully. 'I don't know what to wish for, and that's a fact,' he said slowly. 'It seems to me I've got all I want.'

'If only the house was paid for, you'd be quite happy, wouldn't you!' said Herbert, with his hand on his shoulder. 'Well, wish for two hundred pounds, then; that'll just do it.'

His father, smiling, held up the paw. His son winked at

1 small gift

his mother, sat down at the piano, and struck a few impressive chords.

'I wish for two hundred pounds,' said the old man distinctly.

A fine crash from the piano greeted the words, interrupted by a shuddering cry from the old man. His wife and son ran toward him.

'It moved,' he cried, with a glance of disgust at the object as it lay on the floor. 'As I wished, it twisted in my hand like a snake.'

'Well, I don't see the money,' said his son, as he picked it up and placed it on the table, 'and I bet I never shall.'

'It must have been your imagination,' said his wife.

He shook his head. 'Never mind, though; there's no harm done, but it gave me a shock all the same.'

They sat down by the fire again. Outside, the wind was higher than ever, and the old man jumped nervously at the sound of a door banging upstairs. A silence, unusual and depressing, settled upon all three, which lasted until the old couple arose to retire for the night.

'I expect you'll find the cash tied up in a big bag in the middle of your bed,' said Herbert, as he bade them goodnight, 'and something horrible sitting up on top of the dresser watching you as you pocket your ill-gotten gains.'

He sat alone in the darkness, gazing at the dying fire and seeing faces in it. The last face was so horrible that he gazed at it in amazement. It got so vivid that, with a little uneasy laugh, he felt on the table for a glass containing a little water to throw over it. His hand grasped the monkey's paw, and with a little shiver he wiped his hand on his coat and went up to bed.

In the brightness of the wintry sun next morning as it streamed over the breakfast table, he laughed at his fears.

'I suppose all old soldiers are the same,' said Mrs White. 'The idea of our listening to such nonsense! How could wishes be granted in these days? And if they could, how could two hundred pounds hurt you, father?'

'Might drop on his head from the sky,' said Herbert jokingly.

'Morris said the things happened so naturally,' said his father, 'that you might think it was only coincidence.'

'Well, don't break into the money before I come back,' said Herbert as he rose from the table. 'I'm afraid it'll turn you into a mean, greedy man, and we shall have to disown you.'

His mother laughed and, following him to the door, watched him down the road.

'Herbert will have some more of his funny remarks, I expect, when he comes home,' she said.

'I dare say,' said Mr White, 'but for all that, the thing moved in my hand; that I'll swear to.'

'You thought it did,' said the old lady soothingly.

'I *say* it did,' replied the other. 'There was no thought about it.'

His wife made no reply.

In the late afternoon Mrs White was watching the mysterious movements of a man outside, who, peering in an undecided fashion at the house, appeared to be trying to make up his mind to enter. In thinking about the two hundred pounds, she noticed that the stranger was well dressed. Three times he paused at the gate, and then walked on again. The fourth time he stood with his hand upon it, and then suddenly flung it open and walked up the path. Mrs White went to the door and brought the stranger, who seemed ill at ease, into the room. He gazed at her, and listened in a preoccupied[1] fashion as the old lady apologized for the appearance of the room. She then waited as patiently as she could for him to state his business, but he was at first strangely silent.

1 thinking about something else

'I – was asked to call,' he said at last. 'I come from Maw and Meggins.'

The old lady started. 'Is anything the matter?' she asked breathlessly. 'Has anything happened to Herbert? What is it? What is it?'

Her husband interrupted. 'There, there, mother,' he said hastily. 'Sit down, and don't jump to conclusions. You've not brought bad news, I'm sure, sir.'

'I'm sorry –' began the visitor.

'Is he hurt?' demanded the mother wildly.

The visitor bowed in assent. 'Badly hurt,' he said quietly, 'but he is not in any pain.'

'Oh, thank God!' said the old woman clasping her hands. 'Thank God for that! Thank –'

She broke off suddenly as the sinister meaning of his words dawned upon her. She caught her breath and turning to her slower-witted husband, laid a trembling old hand upon his. There was a long silence.

'He was caught in the machinery,' said the visitor in a low voice.

'Caught in the machinery,' repeated Mr White, in a dazed fashion.

He sat staring blankly out at the window and took his wife's hand into his own.

'He was the only one left to us,' he said, turning gently to the visitor. 'It is hard.'

The other coughed and, rising, walked slowly to the window. 'The firm wished me to convey their sincere sympathy to you in your great loss,' he said, without looking round.

There was no reply. The old woman's face was white, her eyes staring.

'I am to say that Maw and Meggins disclaim all responsibility,' continued the other. 'They admit no liability at all, but in consideration of your son's services, they wish to present you with a certain sum as compensation.'

Mr White dropped his wife's hand and, rising to his feet,

gazed with a look of horror at his visitor. His dry lips shaped the words, 'How much?'

'Two hundred pounds,' was the answer.

Unconscious of his wife's shriek, the old man smiled faintly, put out his hands like a sightless man, and dropped, a senseless heap, to the floor.

In the huge new cemetery, some two miles distant, the old people buried their dead and came back to the house steeped in shadow and silence. It was all over so quickly that at first they could hardly realize it. Sometimes they hardly exchanged a word, for now they had nothing to talk about, and their days were long and weary.

It was about a week after that the old man, waking suddenly in the night, stretched out his hand and found himself alone. The room was in darkness, and the sound of weeping came from the window. He raised himself in bed and listened.

'Come back,' he said tenderly. 'You will be cold.'

'It is colder for my son,' said the old woman, and she wept afresh.

The sound of her sobs died away on his ears. The bed was warm, and his eyes heavy with sleep. He slept until a sudden wild cry from his wife awoke him with a start.

'The paw!' she cried wildly. 'The monkey's paw!'

He started up in alarm. 'Where? Where is it? What's the matter?'

She came stumbling across the room toward him. 'I want it,' she said quietly. 'You've not destroyed it?'

'It's in the parlour,' he replied. 'Why?'

'I only just thought of it,' she said hysterically.[1] 'Why didn't I think of it before? Why didn't *you* think of it?'

'Think of what?' he questioned.

'The other two wishes,' she replied rapidly. 'We've had one.'

1 crying wildly

62

'Was not that enough?' he demanded fiercely.

'No,' she cried, 'we'll have one more. Go down and get it quickly, and wish our boy alive again.'

The man sat up in bed and flung the covers off. 'Good God, you are mad!' he cried, aghast.

'Get it,' she panted; 'get it quickly, and wish – Oh, my boy, my boy!'

Her husband struck a match and lit the candle. 'Get back to bed,' he said unsteadily. 'You don't know what you are saying.'

'We had the first wish granted,' said the old woman feverishly. 'Why not the second?'

'A coincidence,' stammered the old man.

'Go and get it and wish,' cried his wife, quivering with excitement.

The old man's voice shook. 'He has been dead ten days, and besides he – I would not tell you else, but – I could only recognize him by his clothing. If he was too terrible for you to see then, how now?'

'Bring him back,' cried the old woman and dragged him toward the door. 'Do you think I fear my own child?'

He went down in the darkness, and felt his way to the parlour. The paw was in its place. A horrible fear that the unspoken wish might bring his mutilated[1] son before him sooner than he could escape from the room seized upon him, and he caught his breath as he found that he had lost the direction of the door. His brow cold with sweat, he felt his way round the table and groped along the wall until he found himself in the small passage with the ugly thing in his hand.

Even his wife's face seemed changed as he entered the room. It was white and he was afraid of her.

'Wish!' she cried, in a strong voice.

'It is foolish and wicked,' he said.

'Wish!' repeated his wife.

1 maimed

He raised his hand. 'I wish my son alive again.'

The paw fell to the floor, and he looked at it fearfully. Then he sank trembling into a chair as the old woman, with burning eyes, walked to the window and raised the blind.

He sat until he was chilled with the cold, glancing occasionally at the figure of the old woman peering through the window. The old man, with an unspeakable sense of relief at the failure of the paw, crept back to his bed, and a minute or two afterward the old woman came to his side.

Neither spoke, but listened silently to the ticking of the clock. A stair creaked, and a squeaky mouse scurried noisily through the wall. The darkness was heavy, and after lying for some time gathering up his courage, he took the box of matches and, striking one, went downstairs for a candle.

At the foot of the stairs, the match went out, and he paused to strike another. At the same moment a knock, so quiet as to be scarcely audible,[1] sounded on the front door.

The matches fell from his hand and spilled in the passage. He stood motionless, his breath suspended until the knock was repeated. Then he turned and fled swiftly back to his room and closed the door behind him. A third knock sounded through the house.

'What's that?' cried the old woman, starting up.

'A rat,' said the old man in shaking tones – 'a rat. It passed me on the stairs.'

His wife sat up in bed listening. A loud knock resounded through the house.

'It's Herbert!' she screamed. 'It's Herbert!'

She ran to the door, but her husband was before her and, catching her by the arm, held her tightly.

'What are you going to do?' he whispered hoarsely.

'It's my boy; it's Herbert!' she cried, struggling. 'I forgot it was two miles away. What are you holding me for? Let go. I must open the door.'

1 loud enough to be heard

'For God's sake, don't let it in,' cried the old man, trembling.

'You're afraid of your own son,' she cried struggling. 'Let me go. I'm coming, Herbert; I'm coming!'

There was another knock, and another. The old woman with a sudden wrench broke free and ran from the room. Her husband followed to the landing and called after her as she hurried downstairs. He heard the chain rattle back and the bottom bolt drawn slowly and stiffly from the socket. Then the old woman's voice, strained and panting:

'The bolt,' she cried loudly. 'Come down. I can't reach it.'

But her husband was on his hands and knees groping wildly on the floor in search of the paw. If he could only find it before the thing outside got in. The knocks echoed through the house, and he heard the scraping of a chair as his wife put it down in the passage against the door. He heard the creaking of the bolt as it came slowly back, and at the same moment he found the monkey's paw, and frantically[1] breathed his third and last wish.

The knocking ceased suddenly, although the echoes of it were still in the house. He heard the chair drawn back, and the door opened. A cold wind rushed up the staircase. A long, loud wail of disappointment and misery from his wife gave him courage to run down to her side, and then to the gate beyond. The street lamp shone on a quiet and deserted road.

1 madly

Gaffer Roberts

John Griffin

If my Mam got mad with me for something I'd done – or more often something I hadn't done – she used to make moaning noises and stagger about the house as if she was dying. My Dad used to say, 'Now look what you've done to your mother,' and if I answered back, he would start pelting[1] things at me – plates, cups, his dinner, the carving knife and once a picture of Jesus floating up to heaven with a lamb tucked under each arm.

When he started his pelting I ran, either to my bedroom upstairs or to the toilet at the bottom of the garden. Both places had latches and as long as I got ten yards' start on him, I could slam the door shut and slip my half clothes-peg under the latch – I always carried a half clothes-peg for the purpose – and no matter how much he blasphemed[2] and kicked at the door he couldn't get in.

One Monday morning I lay in bed looking out of my skylight window at nothing in particular; there wasn't anything to see except sky because the window was merely a hole in the roof which you could open or shut with a long wooden handle. I had to sleep with it closed because if I left it open the cat would jump in and more likely than not land from ten feet on to my face – a nasty way to wake up. Anyway this particular Monday morning I didn't feel like getting up although my Mam had already shouted: 'If he

1 throwing, hurling
2 cursed

66

thinks he's going to have me at his beck and call just to get him his breakfast when he wants, he's got another think coming.' She never addressed me directly when she was mad.

When I eventually got downstairs she said to my Dad, 'Tell him his breakfast's in the oven if he wants it.' I was feeling pretty fed up but I shouldn't have said what I did.

'Tell her to stuff her head in the oven.'

I know it wasn't very witty but it certainly galvanized[1] my Dad.

'Right, you great wammock,' he shouted and looked round for something to pelt. I was still a bit sleepy and I hesitated a moment, not knowing whether to run to the bog or the bedroom. The last time I'd made for the bog he'd broken my back when he caught me straight between the shoulder blades with a loaf of bread. If you think that wouldn't hurt, I'd better tell you it was one of Albert Rowe's specials – stale and very crusty.

Anyway that thought decided me to make for the bedroom but I was late starting and had only just reached the top of the stairs when he was half-way up with the big brown teapot held in his pelting position. I wasn't going to make it! I couldn't possibly get the peg in the door before he got his foot in it. I turned to face him. He stopped. Neither of us knew what to do. Then he put his head down, growled and took the last few stairs three at a time. Just as he reached the top step I gave him a push – not a hard push, just defensive. He lost his balance and he and the teapot clattered downstairs. He reached the bottom first and the teapot, a close second, hit him on the head and smashed, spilling luke-warm tea down his navy-blue shirt. He looked up at me with a scowl, a scowl of surprise. I looked down at him in astonishment. It was a significant[2] moment. Neither of us spoke. He picked up the broken pot and went away.

1 excited
2 important

After that he still chased me, firing away with Wellington boots, sugar bowls and other unlikely weapons. But both of us knew he didn't intend catching me. We both went a bit slower. What used to be a real chase had become a ritual. I had become as strong as my Dad.

I'm telling you all this about my Dad because in a peculiar way it helps to explain in my mind the downfall of Gaffer Roberts.

I used to hate meeting Gaffer Roberts when I was a boy. Even before I was five he used to plague me with questions. I would be walking home with my Dad after singling beet[1] or something and meet Gaffer coming out of school. He was headmaster of the village school, a matchstick man with a bent back – as if one of the matches had slipped forward – and a rusty face; he had some disease that made his skin go rusty.

'Afternoon, Fred,' Gaffer would say to my Dad.

'Afternoon, suh,' my Dad would say.

'So this is the youngster, is it, Fred? Let's see, how old will he be now?'

I always managed to tell him my age but that was about the limit of my side of the conversation with Gaffer.

'Now, young man, I've got a sixpence, a threepenny bit and six pennies in my pocket. How much does that make?'

When Gaffer first asked me that sort of question I thought he was bragging about his wealth so I said, 'Very good,' or something like that, but I noticed it didn't go down very well. Later I learnt that no sums teacher can ask you a straightforward question. They always have to go on about Bill Smith setting out to walk somewhere or Joe Brown filling his bath, instead of just asking the volume of water in a container. I think it's supposed to make it more interesting having Joe Browns and Bill Smiths in it.

I got very few of Gaffer's sums right. The more he asked the worst I got. It was his head that put me off when he bent

1 thinning out sugar-beet plants

down to ask his questions. You see he'd only got a big tuft of black hair in the middle of his head but he used it carefully, spreading it out from the centre to all parts of his head and keeping it plastered down with Brylcreem.[1] As there wasn't enough to cover his head properly he had wide partings to disguise his baldness. Two wide partings ran from front to back and two from side to side. When he bent down to ask me questions his head just looked as if it had been set out for a game of noughts and crosses. And that's what put me off! When he started on about his half-crowns in his waistcoat I tried to concentrate, but I just couldn't stop myself playing mental noughts and crosses on his head. Once I beat myself and got a row of noughts down the right hand side of his head and I gave myself a small grin of triumph.

'There's nothing to laugh at, young man,' said Gaffer in a nasty way, as if he'd been saying things like 'Wipe that grin off your face' for years. 'You'll find a sound basic knowledge of mathematics essential for life, essential.' Gaffer emphasized the point by tapping me on the head.

My Dad was mad with me when Gaffer had matchsticked his way down the road.

'It's pity he's retiring; he'd sort you and the rest of the young devils out, would old Gaffer. He nearly killed your Uncle Jack with a walking-stick because he was late for school one morning.'

My Dad went on and on about how fierce Old Gaffer was and how there ought to be more teachers like him about.

'He's only sixty-two; he's still got a lot of life in him. Nobody messed about in Gaffer's school.'

I was surprised Gaffer was only sixty-two; he looked more like a hundred and sixty-two to me, but I was quite impressed by what my Dad said about him and whenever I saw Gaffer after I tried to hide so that he didn't see me. I was pretty scared of him.

1 hair-grease

It was several years later and I was in the top class at the village school. Fatty Heathershaw, Woolly Lamb and Skulker were in the same class despite being older than me. You see if you didn't pass to go to the school in town you stayed at the village school until you were fourteen. We were a pretty rowdy lot and the Headmaster, Silas Rudkin, had a job to keep us in order. One morning he ran off with the dinner and bank money. He didn't get very far – to his sister's in Newark – so the police found him by Friday and got most of the thirty pounds back. It was then that they gave out that he'd had what they called a nervous breakdown and that it was caused by 'pressure of work'. I didn't know whether we were the 'pressure of work' but I'm sure we must have been part of it at least.

They couldn't get a new teacher for the next few weeks so they got Gaffer to come out of his retirement. The Vicar came to tell us the news just before we went home on Friday. I wasn't very pleased and neither were most of the others. We all knew Gaffer's reputation and felt we had to be on our best behaviour.

The first three days all went quite well. We sat and listened to Old Gaffer going on about verbs and Pythagoras and capital towns. It was a good job Old Gaffer's reputation was so strong because he was even more boring than Silas Rudkin.

'Please, sir,' said Skulker on the Thursday morning when Gaffer was going on about tin-mining in Bolivia, 'can I go to the toilet?'

'Yes, I suppose you are able to,' said Gaffer with a sarcastic grin. Skulker got up and shambled to the door.

'Where are you going, boy?'

'To the toilet, sir.'

'I said I presumed you were able to go to the toilet. If you are asking my permission to go the answer is no, certainly not.' Gaffer sat back with a grin of triumph on his face.

None of us had a clue what he was talking about and the next half-hour he bored us silly going on about the difference between 'can' and 'may' and smirking all the time as if he'd outsmarted us.

At break we turned on Skulker, saying it was his fault for asking to go to the toilet. Skulker didn't see that it was his fault; neither did we actually but as we daren't get at Gaffer Roberts we had to blame somebody and Skulker seemed the best target. In the end Skulker said, 'I'll fix him after break.'

We sneered at this; Skulker only dared to muck about when everybody else was. This time we had underestimated him though.

After break Gaffer started on measuring fields in acres and rods[1] and that sort of thing.

'A farmer wants to plant a field of wheat,' said Gaffer, 'but he doesn't know how much seed to buy. So he goes into the field and starts to measure down one side in yards. The first side measures . . .'

'What if there's a bull in it?' shouted Skulker. There was a frozen silence. I looked at Skulker with interest, wondering what sort of corpse he would make and how long it would take to clear the blood up. I think we were all amazed, even Skulker, when Old Gaffer pretended not to hear him and picked up the thread of his sum.

'Down the first side he measures eighty-seven yards,' said Gaffer, 'and down the next side he measures . . .'

'Yes, but what if there's a bull in the field?' shouted Skulker, so loudly that he couldn't be ignored.

Gaffer put down his chalk. 'This is it!' I thought. 'We'll have to find a new goalkeeper for the football team.' Skulker was a rotten goalie anyway, doing great acrobatic dives after the ball was in the net.

'Who are you, boy?'

'Wheat,' said Skulker in a hoarse whisper.

'Come here, Wheat. I'm going to have to thrash you.' Skulker didn't move.

1 unit of measure

71

'Come here,' shouted Old Gaffer in a loud but panicky sort of voice. Skulker sat down.

Then Gaffer went towards him and suddenly started clipping Skulker round the ears and hair with both hands. But it was obvious from the start that he wasn't hurting Skulker at all. After about a minute Old Gaffer was breathing heavily; he was about all in. He went back and sat in his chair.

Nothing more was said that lesson but the writing was on the wall for Old Gaffer. Next morning we had Religious Knowledge. Each boy had to read a verse from the Bible one after the other round the form. Well, Fatty Heathershaw started reading his verse. When he'd finished I started mine; the only trouble for Old Gaffer was that Fatty started to read his again and when I'd finished Woolly started his and Fatty and I started ours again. It was quite easy if you kept your head down and concentrated on reading your verse louder than anybody else. As the noise and babble increased Old Gaffer started to shout, 'Stop, stop it at once,' but soon he couldn't make himself heard. He started to run up and down the rows shouting into each boy's ear, telling him to stop. When he did this you stopped for a few seconds and then started up again when he went further down the row. With Silas Rudkin we'd got up to fifteen people reading different verses at once, until he managed to stop us by hitting each of the readers on the head with a metal ruler.

With Old Gaffer we got twenty-two reading before the bell rang for break. That stopped us.

'You louts, you fools, you wait,' was all Gaffer managed to say.

'You said each one read a verse,' shouted Woolly. Gaffer got up and walked out. Friday was fairly quiet after that. We knew we'd won and didn't want to make a fuss about it; after all he was an old bloke.

He didn't turn up the next Monday and old Mrs Armitage had us with her class. We got on all right there.

72

She wasn't too bad and we didn't muck about. I don't know why we didn't muck about with her. We just didn't; we didn't seem to want to annoy her somehow.

Old Gaffer didn't come back again and I began to feel sorry for him. But after a time I felt it served him right. If you scare people by hitting them then one day they'll be able to get you; it stands to reason. Anyway, he shouldn't have been sarcastic[1] and smart; him and his 'may I' and 'can I' and all that clever nonsense.

1 mocking

The Outside Chance

Jan Carew

It's a funny thing about money. If you haven't got it, you think it's the most important thing in the world. That's what I used to think, too. I don't any more, though, and I learned the hard way.

When I was at school, we had this English master. He was always quoting to us from famous writers. I wasn't very interested, and I don't remember much about it now. But it's funny how things come back to you. He used to say:

'When the gods wish to punish us, they answer our prayers.'

Sounds a bit daft, doesn't it? Well, I didn't understand it then, either, but I can tell you what it means now. It means if you want something really badly, you'll probably get it. But you'll probably get it in a way you don't expect.

I mean, you might have to pay a price you didn't bargain for.

It started one rainy day, when I was coming home from work.

I'm a motor mechanic, and I liked working in the garage. But, I was restless. I'd always had this dream of owning my own business. Nothing big – just something I could build up. I don't mind hard work, you see, if I'm working for myself. That's why I'd left my mum and dad in the North, and come to London. I thought I'd make more money that way.

We'd had arguments about it. My dad and me. He didn't see why I should want to leave home when I had enough to live on.

Enough! Enough for what? I used to ask him. To live as he had in a council house all his life, with nothing to look forward to but a gold watch and a pension?

Oh, I was fond of him, you see, and it annoyed me to see him so content. He had nothing to show for all those years of work in that noisy factory.

Anyway, all this was on my mind, as I walked home that night. The rain didn't help, either. I remember thinking, if only I could get out of the rut, if only I could get a thousand quid – just that, just a thousand.

I stopped and bought a newspaper outside the Tube. I thought it would take my mind off things on the way home. I could read about other people's troubles for a change. See what films were on.

I don't know when I first realised there was something wrong with the paper. It looked ordinary enough. But there was something about it that didn't seem quite right. As if there was a gap in the news. As if it was a jump ahead. So, in the end, I looked at the front page, and instead of Tuesday 22nd November, it said Wednesday 23rd November.

'My God,' I thought, 'it's tomorrow's paper!'

I didn't believe it to start with. But it did explain why all the news was different. There couldn't be any other explanation. Somehow, I had bought tomorrow's paper – today!

And that was the moment I realised it. The moment I realised that all my prayers could be answered. My hands were shaking so much that I could hardly turn the pages. But they *were* there. The results of tomorrow's races!

I looked at the winners, and chose from them carefully. I picked only the outsiders that had won at prices like 30–1.

75

There was even one at 50–1! A horse I would never have thought of betting on.

Next morning, I went to the bank, and drew out just about all I had – £150. I laid my bets during my lunch hour. I went to several shops. I didn't want anyone to become suspicious.

It's a funny thing, but I just knew they'd come up. And – God forgive me – I never stopped to think *why* I had been given this chance to see into the future.

They *did* come up – every one of them. All I had to do was to go round and collect, and I couldn't wait to get home and count my money. A cool £4,000!!

Well, nothing could stop me now! I'd give in my notice at work the next day, and look for a place of my own. Wait till I told Mum and Dad! They'd hardly be able to believe it.

I switched on the television, but I couldn't concentrate on it. I kept thinking what I'd do with the money. I hardly heard a word of the programme.

Then the news came on.

The announcer mentioned Selby. That was where my parents lived. I began to listen.

There had been an explosion up there, that afternoon, followed by a fire in a factory. Twenty-two people had been killed, and many more were in hospital. I don't remember the rest – something about a government enquiry.

I stopped listening, but I couldn't move out of the chair. I think I must've known then that my dad was dead – even before the telegram came.

The newspaper had fallen on the floor. I picked it up, not realising what I was doing. Then, I saw it – in the 'Stop Press'. FACTORY DISASTER IN SELBY. MANY FEARED DEAD. I hadn't seen it before. I'd been too busy picking winners. I could've saved my dad's life, but I'd been too busy picking bloody winners. I don't often cry, but the words swam in front of me then.

There isn't much more to tell. I got my own business, and I'm doing well. As for my Mum, she was paid insurance by the firm that owned the factory, so she's better off than she ever was. The only thing is, she doesn't care if she's alive or dead now my Dad's gone.

When the gods wish to punish us, they make a damn good job of it.

The Wild Geese

· Emil Pacholek

The lands of Kincaple flowed gently from the high grounds of Strathkinness, down and down in a run of green and gradual undulations.[1]

The farm itself, a clutter of old, sandstone buildings, had been built into the slope of the last of the waves of hills, then below it, the ground spread itself flat and wide and fertile, right down to the marshlands that skirted the River Eden.

It was in one of the bottom fields, the one that was nearest to the fringes of whispering reeds and rushes, that Robbie and McPhee built the hide.

They'd worked well that Sunday, trailing long branches down from the Den Wood across the stubble field. It was hard and heavy going, and the field was wet with late October dampness.

Their leather boots were soaked and heavy, but they'd long since stopped caring about that.

The plan! That was all that mattered! That was all they thought about . . .

They rammed the bigger branches on end into the clay ground, in a rough circle just big enough to hold the pair of them. Then, in between the main branches, they threaded smaller ones, and reeds and clumps of grass, leaving but a small entrance gap to wriggle into, and a couple of little slits to peep out of!

1 land shaped like waves

All morning it took them, and well into the afternoon. But it was worth it. The hide was near perfect.

'Can you see in?' called Robbie in a coarse whisper to McPhee, who stood outside.

'Not a sign of you!' came the tinker boy's hushed reply.

It was strange them whispering, for the whole field was empty but for the pair of them, and the nearest houses were across the estuary in Guardbridge, over a mile away!

But dark deeds were afoot, and secrecy was all important.

'What about the grain?' whispered McPhee.

'There's a bin in the stables with loads of the stuff,' said Robbie. 'I'll get a bagful on my way back.'

'And the . . . the . . .' McPhee paused to look around before he dared say the word. His dark eyes shone with the devilment. 'And the whisky?'

Robbie grinned.

'My mother has some in the press. I'll get it tonight.'

'So it's tonight then?' asked McPhee.

Robbie looked up at the pale, silver sky. There was no cloud and already a big moon hung up in the east, shining like a half-crown.

'There'll be loads of light tonight. We'll see them fine!'

And so it was arranged.

The plan they'd worked out at the potato picking through the week was ready to be put to the test.

They'd been taking their break together, lying on their backs in the drills[1] in the field up by the Den Wood when they'd come swinging over – the geese!

'It'd be a fine thing getting a couple of them,' Robbie had said, aiming and firing both barrels of an imaginary twelve-bore at the leading bird.

They'd watched the skein[2] circle, lower and lower, cautious, looking out for any sign of danger. Round they

1 rows of seeds
2 flock

went, and again in a wide sweep, but lower and lower all the time. Then, together, the flock had settled down into the barley stubble of the bottom field.

'We'd need some sort of a hide,' McPhee had said. 'Then we could sit in it at night and wait until they were close –'

'And grab them!' Robbie had cried. 'But . . . but they'd rise before we were near . . .'

There was a long silence as they both let the thoughts race through their minds.

'But what if we doped them, somehow,' Robbie had said. 'Then they'd be that bit slower in taking off . . .'

'Aye,' McPhee had said. 'But what could we dope them with . . .?'

The last pieces of the plan had fallen neatly into place. And now they were ready to test it.

'I'll give you a hoot about midnight,' Robbie said as the two boys reached the top corner of the field at the foot of the Den Wood. And with no more than that, they parted. McPhee heading for his tinker's camp in the hollow halfway up the Den, and Robbie back to the stone cottage in the village of Kincaple.

But first through the farm. He had some grain to get.

Robbie slipped quiet as a cat through the farmyard, keeping his body close to the walls, edging up to corners, peeping round then scampering across the open spaces until he was at the stables.

He put his weight against the sliding door, hoping, hoping that the cast-iron wheels wouldn't squeak on the runners and give him away. But no sound came, and when the gap was a few inches wide, he squeezed inside, hauling it quietly closed behind him.

All the horses were in their stalls. Summer days had withered into autumn and were fallen and were gone, days when the Clydesdales[1] had spent their free hours turned loose in the lush, green park at the back of the farm. Days

1 a breed of carthorses

of capering and cantering, and nuzzling friendly like at each other's shoulders where the collars had pressed hard onto them when they'd been toiling through the long hours.

But the grass had lost its sweetness, and the horses had been moved inside, to the warmth of the deep straw, and the rich clover flavour of the hay in the mangers.

Two of the horses tossed their heads to see who the intruder was, but just for a moment, then it was back to tugging at a clump of hay and squeezing the sweet juices from it.

Robbie moved quietly down to the huge bins at the far end of the stable. He tugged at the lid, heaved it open, then dipped his hand inside. It was crushed oats . . . just what he was after!

There was a sack lying near and he picked it up, shaking the stoor[1] from it in a great cloud. The dust tickled at his nose but he fought off the sneeze. No one must find him!

Then he delved a scoop into the bin and poured a cascade of oats into the open mouth of the sack. Then again. And again.

As he dipped in for the fourth time, the voice came from behind him!

'And just what do you think you're up to, laddie?'

Robbie whirled and the scoop flew out of his hand, clattering to the floor and birling[2] on the stone as he gaped, eyes wide, heart hammering.

From out of the end stall, from out of the shadows, came Dauve. Old Dauve, the strange quiet horseman who spent nearly every hour he had in the company of his pair of Clydesdales.

'Well, laddie – have you lost your tongue?'

Robbie's head reeled. The plan – he mustn't reveal the plan!

'It's for – it's for the hens!' he stammered out. 'We've

1 dust
2 spinning

got nothing to feed them on. Can I – can I take a wee bagful?'

Dauve was close now, and his grey eyes stared hard at Robbie. They narrowed. For a long minute, Dauve said nothing. Then he made a sort of snorting noise and nodded.

'Aye, I suppose you can.'

Relief washed through Robbie, and he made to dash off with his plunder, but Dauve plucked the sack from his hand.

'But you'll have to earn this! You'll have to give me a hand with the horses.'

Kincaple Farm had four pairs of Clydesdale horses, and none looked better than Punch and Jeck, the two that old Dauve worked.

Their coats had more of a sheen, their harness more of a shine, and they even appeared to move better, with a self assured swing to their walk that seemed to speak of the respect they had for the man.

It was a handsome sight seeing Dauve at the close of the day, sitting sideways up on Jeck with Punch in right behind, fair full of themselves, a real team and matched just right for each other.

He was a strange sort, dour and sullen, keeping himself to himself. He lived alone in a cramped little bothy[1] in the village, but folks said it was more in the way of being a holiday home for Dauve, and that his real home was down in the stables for it was there that he spent most of his time, grooming his horses, talking to them, and polishing at the brass and leather of the harnesses.

Dauve handed Robbie a rope-handled, wooden bucket.

'You can fill that up with fine sawdust for me,' he said. 'And make sure it's dry stuff, mind!'

Robbie scurried round to the saw bench. The men had been making fence-stabs,[2] and beneath the jagged, circular

1 hut for farmworkers
2 fence-posts

blade was a great mound of white sawdust. The boy delved the bucket into it and filled it to the brim.

When he returned to the stable, Dauve was at his horses. He was bathing their feet, washing the great plumed hooves. When he'd finished, he took handfuls of the sawdust and rubbed it into the long hair, working it right in. Then he brushed it all out and combed each foot in turn.

'What do you do that for?' asked Robbie.

'It dries them,' answered Dauve, picking up each hoof in turn to inspect the hair and the shoe. 'The sawdust dries the hair. Makes a grand like job.'

Dauve picked at a hoof, coaxing[1] out a stone.

'It's all a question of care,' he said. 'You mind that when you're older and you're working a pair of horse for yourself.'

Robbie grinned.

'But it'll not be horse then, Dauve. The farm'll be all tractors by that time.'

Dauve straightened up and for a moment, a strange look seemed to come on him – a far away look, either remembering days gone by or imagining days yet to come, Robbie wasn't sure.

Then Dauve snatched up Robbie's bag of oats and tossed it to him.

'Get away with you,' was all he said.

When he reached his cottage, Robbie didn't go in straight away. Instead, he went into the wash-house next door. He took a pail and poured the crushed oats into it, then hid it behind the fat, black boiler.

Then he gave his boots a quick brush with the broom, stuck his hands deep into his pockets and whistled as he sauntered,[2] all innocent like, round the corner and home.

'And just where on earth have you been?' His mother's

1 easing
2 strolled

words rattled like hail as she met him at the door. 'Nothing inside your belly since breakfast! You'll have been with that McPhee, I'll bet – and up to some mischief or other!'

Robbie made his eyes go wide, and looked up at his mother.

'I've been helping Dauve, Mum,' he said. 'He wanted a hand with his horses.'

Robbie's mother looked hard at him for a moment.

'I'd have thought Dauve was able to look after his horses just fine without your assistance!'

But then, with a light skelp[1] at his head, she smiled.

'Come on,' she said. 'There's some stewed hare in the oven – you're bound to be starving.'

Seconds later, the dish was out of the oven at the side of the fire, and before him, hot and steaming up into his face.

Robbie drew the sweet smell deep inside him, savouring the mouth-watering scent of it all.

'There's nothing to beat stewed hare, Mum,' he said, dipping a chunk of bread into the rich gravy. 'Except maybe,' he added, 'a nice roast goose.'

Robbie smiled a secret little smile to himself.

After he'd shut away the hens for the night, and filled up with sticks and coal, and done all the rest of his chores, Robbie put the final stages of his plan into action.

His mother was sitting by the fire in the living-room, darning a new heel into a sock. She looked up over the top of her spectacles as the boy came through from the kitchen and her eyes opened wide with surprise.

'I've made you some tea!' Robbie announced, pouring what he'd spilt in the saucer back into the cup.

His mother beamed into a smile and shook her head in amazement.

'My, Robbie,' she exclaimed, putting her darning to one side. 'How lovely!'

1 slap

'It's my pleasure, Mum,' declared Robbie grandly.

He sat by the fender, watching his mother sip at the brew. There was sugar in it – she took none – and the water hadn't been brought fully to the boil, giving it a coarse, raw sort of taste that fair scraped at the palate.[1] But his mother said nothing, just sipped at it with a look of pleasure and contentment on her.

'Would you like some more?' Robbie asked when the last of it was gone. His mother shook her head – but not too much.

'No thank you, Robbie – that was just lovely.'

'Well, you bide[2] where you are, Mum, and I'll wash the cup for you.'

And with that, the boy left, closing the door behind him and just missing the smile that tugged at the corners of his mother's mouth.

In the kitchen, Robbie rushed into action.

He eased open the press[3] door and there it was – the whisky bottle! He carried it carefully in two hands over to the table, eased off the cork, and poured its entire contents into a jug.

Then he took the teapot and at the sink, half filled up the empty bottle with tea. Then he topped it up with water until the colour was just right, and rammed the cork back in.

His hands trembled as he slid the whisky bottle back to its place on the shelf in the press.

After that, he took the torch, let himself silently out of the kitchen door, and hurried as much as he dared with the full jug of whisky.

In the wash-house, he poured the whisky into the bucket of crushed oats and was back in the kitchen in seconds,

1 roof of the mouth
2 stay
3 cupboard

85

whistling loudly and rattling at the cup and saucer in the sink.

Unaware of it all, his mother still sat darning in the living-room, sucking at a peppermint, trying to rid her palate of the taste of the tea.

As he lay in bed that night, Robbie's heart seemed to pound away inside him like the mill at threshing time!

The plan! The plan! The plan! His head fairly thundered with the thought of it.

He'd left the curtains open, and outside, the moon rose full and gleaming above the trees, painting all the branches with silver.

It was a fine night. A perfect night. And when he heard the geggle-gaggle calls from a skein of geese, flying over towards the estuary, it seemed to him like it was an omen, and Robbie's heart beat all the faster.

He heard the clock in the lobby strike half past nine, then ten . . .

Nearly an hour later, he heard his mother give the fire its final poke for the night, and a short time later, the door of her room gave a click.

Then silence!

The clock struck eleven-thirty – and Robbie swung out of bed. He put his clothes on over the top of his pyjamas, carried his boots in his hand, eased up the window and was out!

He paused for a moment or two as he tied his laces, listening at the window, but there was no sound from within. Robbie crept into the wash-house, felt for the bucket in the black, found it and was off!

He'd done it!

The sky was scattered with stars and the light from the moon bathed the whole countryside in silver as Robbie ran along the track that led to the Den.

His shadow jiggled[1] like a puppet before him, dancing merrily over the ground.

It seemed as if the whole world was asleep, and when he stopped to rest and change the bucket to his other hand, Robbie heard no sound other than the rush of his own breathing.

The Den Wood lay before him in the hollow like a sleeping dog, growing steadily larger as he loped towards it.

And then he was there!

Robbie cupped his hands to his lips and blew into the gap between his thumbs. His owl-hoot signal carried far into the silent wood, then again.

A few seconds later, an answering hoot came clear, and then McPhee himself was stepping out of the shadows. Under an arm, he carried two sticks.

'All right?' asked McPhee quietly.

'Aye,' Robbie whispered back. 'And yourself?'

'They never heard a thing,' grinned McPhee. 'Come on, let's get going! I've brought a couple of sticks – here's hoping we need them!'

The two boys hurried, crouched low, down the length of the field, keeping close to the line of the hawthorn hedging that ran almost all the way to the riverside.

It seemed as if they could see for miles in the strange light, and soon they could see the outline of their hide down by the reeds.

As they neared it, Robbie suddenly stopped, holding McPhee by the arm.

'Look!' he breathed. 'In the field! Dozens of them!'

McPhee followed the line of Robbie's jabbing finger and there, in the stubble, between the hide and the edge of the rushes, were the plump shapes of a whole flock of greylag geese! Robbie bit at his lip in excitement!

Almost crawling now, the two boys reached the cover of a line of reeds. They eased their way along, moving the pail

1 moved with jerks

a foot or so in front, then wriggling forward. Easing and wriggling . . . easing and wriggling . . .

They were only a few yards away from the safety of their hide now.

Silently, hardly daring to breathe, they stole forward, keeping the hide between themselves and the geese.

And suddenly, they were there!

The two boys squeezed in together, nudging and poking each other in silent delight at their triumph.

McPhee bent back some of the grass from the hide. Robbie dipped into the pail and took out a handful of the mixture. The whisky had soaked right into the crushed oats and its pungent[1] smell filled the hide.

Carefully, so carefully, he tossed a little out onto the stubble before them. Then again. And then some more. If the geese saw the movement, they'd be off and the whole plan ruined! Each handful was a risk they hardly dared take, but luck held, and soon Robbie had emptied the bucket and all the mixture lay in the stubble just a few feet in front of the hide!

The two boys crouched at their peepholes and the long wait began . . .

Outside, the geese cackled softly to each other, some resting with their heads tucked in below their wings, some on guard around the edges of the flocks, and some feeding in the stubble.

But as yet, none fed on the mixture!

It was cold now, and Robbie's legs began to ache.

Although the sky was clear, there was no frost, but the dampness on the ground seemed to seep right into him.

McPhee nudged him on the arm.

'Here!' he whispered in the darkness of the hide, and he fed one of the sticks into Robbie's grip.

Robbie returned to the peephole.

1 sharp, bitter

Some of the geese seemed closer, moving around, foraging[1] in the stubble for food.

One came very near, waddling past less than four feet from them and Robbie saw a quick glint of the moon in its eye, and could make out the lighter colour of its feet and its bill. It didn't eat the oars, didn't even see the stuff, it seemed.

But it was followed by another bird, and this one did see the grain. The goose dipped its head down into the stubble before them and the boys could hear its bill clacking as it tasted the food.

Then again, and this time, it made pleased little noises in its throat as it stretched its neck upwards and ate. Its pleasure was sensed by another goose, and soon, four of them were round the mixture, scooping it up into their bills.

Robbie gripped his fingers into McPhee's arm. McPhee was tense, scarcely breathing.

And still the geese guzzled into the oats, shovelling their bills into it, and it seemed to the two boys that there was a sort of unruliness creeping in.

The birds seemed to be well taken with the stuff.

Was it working? Was it the whisky that was making them greedy, almost reckless to get more? What if they rushed them now?

The questions raced as fast as their pulses.

But no – best to wait . . . give them time . . . let them eat more . . . let them eat the lot!

The two boys watched, dry-mouthed, at their peepholes.

The four geese were almost squabbling with each other, ruffling out their wings, barging at each other, craning their long necks forward, snapping for the food.

It was near time . . .

McPhee tugged at Robbie's sleeve, and silently, stealthily, they crept out of the gap at the rear of the hide.

1 searching

Robbie felt the stick heavy in his hand as they inched round.

Slowly . . . slowly . . . slowly . . .

And then, together, they pounced!

Robbie and McPhee launched themselves forward!

In an instant, the night was filled with alarm calls as scores of wings thrashed the air, pushing, pushing, pushing away from the sudden danger!

Robbie dived to the ground!

Whether it was the whisky, or whether it was the sudden fright that froze it, Robbie never knew – but just as he hit the stubble, his hand fell across a goose's neck! His fingers clasped it instantly!

Robbie felt it come alive in his grip and struggle, and the wings clattered and crashed in panic, cracking him about the head.

But he didn't let go!

His fingers were clamped around the thick neck and were there to stay! Then he swung the stick and felt it thud onto the goose's back, stunning it. And again . . . and again . . .

With both hands now, Robbie gave a quick jerk, pulling at the bird's neck. He felt it give.

The goose fluttered and flapped on its back, but its life was already gone.

As he rose to his feet in triumph, Robbie saw McPhee thrash out at another bird, and it too was taken.

All around them, geese cackled into the night, flickering like witches across the face of the moon.

But two would never rise again.

Robbie and McPhee sent yells of delight into the air around them.

All the way home, Robbie thrilled to the weight of the dead goose in his hand. It was huge and fat and heavy, and with every step, the boy could feel the excitement rush up in him. He'd got a goose, a real live goose – at least, it had been!

He chuckled to himself as he imagined his mother's face in the morning. The best thing would be to put it on the kitchen table for her to find first thing!

Then he could help her pluck it, and singe off the fine feathers that they missed, and prepare it and cook it and carve it . . . his mouth fair watered at the thought!

Robbie coaxed up his window and swung quietly inside, dragging the weight of the goose in after him. He took off his boots and tip-toed through to the kitchen, trailing the great dead bird behind him.

He pushed open the door, and as it swung wide, he saw that the room was bright with light.

Robbie blinked, and saw before him his mother, her arms folded, her face clouded, her foot tapping in time to her temper!

Behind her, was the large, forbidding[1] figure of Sergeant Baxter – the Local Police Force himself!

For what seemed an age, no one moved and no one spoke.

The boy with the dead goose stared up at the woman and the policeman – and the woman and the policeman stared down at the boy with the dead goose!

And then the silence was shattered by Robbie's mother!

'Just what have you been up to?' she shrieked. 'You've had me worried sick! I woke up, went through to your room to make sure you were tucked in and – and nothing!'

Her voice rose and rose until it could rise no more! She paused for breath and started all over again!

'Worried sick, I was! I – I've even been up to the phone-box and poor Sergeant Baxter's come pedalling all the way up here on his bike!'

Robbie swallowed hard, then held out the goose. Its head lay dropped over his arm, and spots of blood dripped like sealing wax from its bill onto the floor.

'Goose?' howled his mother. 'I'll give you goose, my lad!'

1 dangerous, ominous

She lunged forward to grab the boy, but Robbie side-stepped and his mother was left clutching the dead bird by the throat! With a yowl[1], she dropped it to the floor!

Robbie made to jink past her, but she whipped round and caught him by the ear.

Sergeant Baxter cleared his throat and tucked his notebook back into the top pocket of his tunic.

'Ah well, now,' he said to Robbie's mother. 'I see you have the matter well in hand. I'll just be getting down the road again . . .'

He buttoned the top button of his uniform, and cleared his throat again. Then he wiped at his mouth with his hand.

'Aye,' he said, smacking his lips. 'It's a right cold night, is it not . . .?'

Robbie's mother relaxed her grip on the boy's ear and turned to the policeman.

'Oh, Sergeant Baxter,' she said. 'How thoughtless of me. Would you – would you care for a wee dram[2] to warm you up on the journey?'

The sergeant pretended to be surprised at the offer.

'Oh, how kind you are,' he smiled, licking at his lips again. 'Well now, a wee dram sounds like a grand idea . . .'

Robbie, already in fear of the hiding that was sure to come, looked on like a doomed rabbit.

His mother reached into the press for the whisky bottle, uncorked it, and poured a large measure into a glass.

'Your very good health!' declared Sergeant Baxter grandly.

And he tipped the lot down his throat.

Robbie closed his eyes.

1 howl
2 a drop of whisky

92

Follow On
The Short Story

Horror, families, myths, science fiction, sport, neighbours, mystery, travel, school, love, ghosts, Westerns – almost every subject you can think of has been the subject of one short story or another. Today the short story is one of the most popular forms of writing used by professional authors, and many are adapted into plays and films for television and cinema. But what exactly *is* a short story? It can vary in length from just a few hundred words to as many as 10,000; in this volume *The Outside Chance* is the shortest at under 1,000 words while *The Wild Geese* stretches to nearly 5,000.

What characterises the majority of short stories is that, as Roald Dahl once observed, 'there is no time for the sun shining through the pine trees'. In other words, the writer has to pitch the reader straight into the action without wasting too many words setting the scene. The novelist can afford a chapter or two to describe scenery and characters; the short story writer has only a brief space in which to tell his tale and, perhaps, put across a point of view. Certainly with the stories in this volume it is the action which is usually more important than the background setting or the characters, though of course each has a vital part to play.

When you are talking or writing about the stories here – or indeed, when you come to write your own short stories – it is useful to know the meaning of certain basic technical words which are regularly used when discussing fiction of any kind, whether the short story, the novel or a play. Try and familiarise yourself with the following terms:

Plot All of us read through a story because we want to know what happens next and how it will end; the plot refers to the action in a story. When you are writing your own stories you need to work out before you begin at least the outline or 'bones' of the plot. You can add the detail or 'flesh' as you go along, and it is worth remembering that it is sometimes impossible to know what you are going to write until you have actually put the words on the page! Look at *The Outside Chance* for an example of a tale in which it is the *plot* which is the most important concern of the author.

Characters These are the 'inhabitants' of the stories, whether young children, gods, animals, teachers or parents. Sometimes characters are carefully described and established in a short story if an understanding of their particular personality is important to the outcome of the action – Gaffer in *Gaffer Roberts* is a good example of this. In other stories the author will depict characters only briefly so that he can focus attention on the action. Writers also attempt to make us sympathise with or take sides against certain characters, so that when something happens to them in the course of the story our emotions are held and involved – Emil Pacholek, for example, encourages his readers to share in the secrecy of Robbie's plan to kill the geese and to enjoy its success, so that when Robbie is finally caught we naturally sympathise with him.

Setting This refers to the place or period of time in which the story is set. In this collection the settings vary from the days of the ancient Greeks in *Swollen-Foot* to the North-West of England during 1930s in *Harold*. Again, as with characters, setting is an ingredient in a story that can either be sketched in quickly or focused upon in considerable detail by the author. In *The Wild Geese*, for example, picturing clearly in the mind's eye 'the lands of Kincaple' greatly enhances our appreciation of the story as a whole.

Narrator Of course it is the author who actually pens the words, but all stories are told from a particular point of view. The author can pretend that he is one of the characters in the action and tell the story from that person's standpoint; this means that he will be using what is called the 'first-person narration' and adopt the 'I' form throughout the story – *The Holiday* is a clear example. Or the author can stand outside the action and look down on it as a kind of all-seeing observer; this is called 'third-person narration' and characters are referred to by their name or as 'he' or 'she' – Ted Hughes does this in *How the Tortoise Became*. The first-person narration has the advantage of making the story seem personal and immediate, while the third-person style allows the reader to 'see inside' all the characters at once. If you try rewriting any of the stories in this volume in your own version, you will see that you can reshape them quite effectively and easily by changing the narrator or narrative position. As you read more and more short stories it will also become evident that subject matter tends to determine which method of narration is most suitable.

Themes We have said that first and foremost authors write to tell a story and readers read to find out 'what happens next'. But stories often contain ideas or a certain point of view or message in which the author is interested, and in the course of the plot he will – either directly or indirectly – attempt to alert the reader to that particular theme or issue. Bernard Ashley in *Equal Rights* would obviously wish to prompt his readers into thinking about discrimination against girls, while Jan Carew in *The Outside Chance* might want us to reflect seriously on the quirks of coincidence in life.

Style This is something very difficult to define, but it basically refers to the *way* in which a writer structures and tells the story, how he or she balances or brings together characters, plot, setting and underlying theme. A ghost story will obviously need to be told in a slightly different style from a love story, but apart from that consideration, all writers have their own particular idiosyncrasies, habits and tricks of composition. When you are discussing the various styles of the authors in this collection think about some of the following:

– length of sentences and paragraphs; we may need to use longer sentences for detailed descriptions of landscape, but short, sharp sentences when wanting to create tension or suspense.
– attention to detail; *similes* may be used to make a scene more vivid:
  "Robbie slipped quiet as a cat through the farmyard.'
  'Robbie's heart seemed to pound away inside him like the mill at threshing time!'
  'His shadow jiggled like a puppet before him.' (*The Wild Geese*)
– how the writer establishes the mood and atmosphere of the tale.
– the opening and closing sentences of a story; does the writer save up a surprise ending?

95

- how the writer makes us laugh.
- where the writer wants us to focus our attention or our sympathies.
- the use of dialogue.
- the use of language more generally; for example, dialect speech in *Harold* or the formal warning language of Apollo in *Swollen-Foot*.

Points for discussion and writing

Equal Rights

This is a previously unpublished short story by one of today's most popular children's novelists. First and foremost, it has a strong, witty storyline, but it also has some serious and thought-provoking points to make. One of the main questions it seems to be asking is whether we have always to accept things exactly as they are in life. Can one person, if only in a small way, help change established opinions and attitudes? Through one particular girl's experiences the author will perhaps make us think about the way girls and boys – and women and men as adults – are treated differently. Some of you may well find yourselves identifying closely with the girl who wants to earn some extra money, but who will not allow herself to be exploited by a local shopkeeper. Bobby's unwitting help adds a neat twist to the action.

1. Why does the shopkeeper allow only two children at a time into his shop? Do your local shops have the same rules? Do customers obey them?
2. Why doesn't the shopkeeper 'recognise business' when he sees the girl?
3. Explain the joke about the *Sun* and the *Beano* made by the man with the briefcase. Why does the shopkeeper not laugh?
4. How does the girl know how much the boys are paid for delivering the papers?

5. What is your impression of the shopkeeper as a person? Can you think of someone like him that you know?
6. Why does he think he can offer the girl less money for the job? Would you have turned down the work?
7. What other ways of earning money does the girl usually try at different times of the year?
8. Mrs Dawson appears to be rather too trusting, letting her baby go out with someone who just calls at her door. What is your reaction to this? What identifies the girl for Mrs Dawson?
9. In what ways is Bobby important to the whole story?
10. What link does the shopkeeper make between the girl and Bobby?
11. What do we learn about Mr Dawson in the story? Can we judge a person's character by what he or she reads?
12. Why does the shopkeeper have 'a green grin' on his face when he offers the girl a copy of *Pop Today*?
13. Describe the various reactions of the shopkeeper to the girl in the course of the story. Why does he finally change his mind and pay her more money?
14. What do you think the author wants us to consider by finishing the story in the way he does? What might he be saying about how attitudes and prejudices are formed in our everyday lives?
15. Look at the way Bernard Ashley tells the story through the girl's eyes, using lots of colloquial everyday expressions. What does this contribute to the story?
16. What does the phrase 'equal rights' mean to you? What other human rights do people talk about and often struggle to achieve? You may like to look up in the library the Universal Declaration of Human Rights adopted by the United Nations in 1948.
17. Discuss occasions when you think girls or boys are discriminated against unfairly. Do girls and boys receive equal rights in your school? Try holding a debate on the subject – you will need to write down a series of notes to start with.
18. Would you like to have the girl in the story as a friend or a sister? Give the reasons for your answer.
19. Having turned down the paper-round, the girl says she

'really needed a bit of money coming in'. What sorts of jobs have you done to earn quick money? Have you ever taken on a job for which you knew you were being unfairly paid? Write about it.

20. Divide a page into two columns: make a list of the advantages and disadvantages of having a part-time job.

21. Write about an occasion when you had to make a fuss to get what you wanted, either from friends, parents or someone you did a job for.

22. Carry out a survey on part-time jobs done by members of your class or by their brothers and sisters. List the different types of work and how much they are paid. Which is the best paid? Which is the worst to do? How many of the jobs are 'unofficial'?

23. Make up an incident about an angry shopkeeper and his customers. Write it either as a play or short story.

Further Reading

Bernard Ashley has written several novels for children which you may like to read: *The Trouble with Donovan Croft*, *Terry on the Fence*, *All My Men*, *A Kind of Wild Justice*, *Break in the Sun* (filmed by BBC Television), and *Dodgem*.

Swollen-Foot

As background to this story, it is important to understand the significance to the Ancient Greeks of their many gods and goddesses. The Greeks believed that various gods ruled different aspects of their everyday lives, among them Artemis, the goddess of the hunt and the moon; Eros, the god of love; Ares, the god of war; Athena, the goddess of wisdom; Nemesis, the goddess of fate and vengeance; and, above them all, Zeus the King of the gods. We might think that all the myths and legends that were told about the gods were just silly superstition, but for the Greeks they helped explain all kinds of natural events from birth to death. They believed that Fate governed their lives, and that what the gods destined for an individual was certain to happen. *Swollen-Foot* is the retelling of one celebrated legend about Oedipus, King of Thebes, 'father-murderer, mother-husband', who struggles in vain to escape his destiny. His bloody, tragic end was the sure fate of any man who tried to prove the gods wrong.

1. We are told in the opening paragraphs what is going to happen in the story. What do you think is the point of beginning in this way? Does it add to or spoil your enjoyment of the tale?
2. Where does the baby gets its name from?
3. Why do you think Jocasta and Laius decide to put an end to their child by leaving him on the mountainside? Why do they not kill him themselves? Find out and compare how the citizens of the city of Sparta in ancient Greece treated their new-born babies.
4. How does the visitor from Thebes (page 7) know that Oedipus is not the real son of Polybos and his queen?
5. Why does Oedipus set off to see *Apollo* at *Delphi*? Find out the importance of these to the Greeks.
6. In what ways does Oedipus misunderstand Apollo's words?
7. The man Oedipus kills at the crossroads is wearing 'a crown of laurel leaves'. What did this signify about a person in ancient Greece?
8. 'You may be Oedipus, and know this answer, but there will be other questions for you one day. Will you know those answers, too?' (page 9). How do these words from the Monster connect with later events (and words) in the story?
9. Explain why Apollo sends a plague to torment the city of Thebes. Can you think of other famous stories in history – in the Bible, for example – when plagues have descended upon a city or people?
10. What is it that causes Jocasta to guess the truth about Oedipus?
11. Why do you think Oedipus blinds himself?
12. 'When the gods send a warning, no man can prove them wrong' (page 13). What does this story tell us about the attitude of the ancient Greeks towards their gods and goddesses?
13. Outline the main events of the story to show how one thing leads inevitably to another.

14. We might think many of the story's incidents are too far-fetched. Write down the things which you find hard to believe.

15. 'Alone, blind, leaning on a stick, Oedipus stumbled out of Thebes.' Continue the story . . .

16. *Swollen-Foot* is told by an outside narrator looking down on all the events. Imagine *you* are Oedipus and rewrite the story from his point of view. Remember from the notes above that you will need to use 'I' throughout your version.

17. Imagine you are a reporter on the *Thebes Gazette*. Write a short account for your newspaper, bearing in mind the shock and horror the people of Thebes would have felt. Think up a striking headline and a drawing to go with the report.

18. Compare *Swollen-Foot* with *The Outside Chance* (page 74). Write down any similarities between the two stories.

19. The riddle about Mankind, which Oedipus solves, is a famous one you may have heard before. Do you know any other riddles? Try them out on others in your class.

20. The riddle about Mankind speaks of three stages in our lives. Do you know Shakespeare's Seven Ages of Man? Look them up in his play *As You Like It*, Act Two.

Further Reading

Having read this story you may want to find out more about Greek myths and legends and do a project on the subject. You could start by reading *The Robe of Blood* by Kenneth McLeish, a collection of stories from which *Swollen-Foot* is taken. It includes the stories of Narcissus, the beautiful boy who fell in love with his own reflection; of King Midas, who turned everything he touched to gold; and of Icarus, who was punished by the gods for flying too near the sun. Other interesting retellings of the Greek myths can be found in *The God Beneath the Sea* and *The Golden Shadow* by Leon Garfield and Edward Blishen.

The Holiday

This story comes from a collection by George Layton in which he describes many different events and adventures which happened in the course of one boy's childhood and adolescence. In fact they are based on the author's own childhood, which makes the stories seem very natural and realistic: the 'I' in *The Holiday* is therefore both the boy narrator and George Layton himself as a child. He obviously remembers his schooldays very vividly and, in particular, the time when he tried desperately to persuade his mother to let him go camping with the other boys – only to discover that it wasn't at all what he had hoped for. In other stories he tells of his grandad's last days; of a meeting with his hero, football-star Bobby Charlton; of a firework display that went disastrously wrong; and of his first date with a girl.

1. At the beginning of the story, the boy seems to know in advance just what his mother is going to say to him. How is he able to do this, do you think? Discuss occasions when you have done this, perhaps with parents or teachers. Write about one particularly memorable incident.

2. What do you imagine is the worst part for the boy of holidaying with his mother and Auntie Doreen each year? Write a description of Mrs Sharkey's boarding house and its guests.

3. What does the boy mean by 'I'll report you to that RSPCC thing' (page 15)?

4. The boy tries to persuade his mother by telling her that Tony's and Barry's parents are letting them go camping. Think of times when you have tried to 'blackmail' your parents in the same way. Were you successful? Did you have any regrets afterwards?

5. 'Honest, what's the point of going on holiday if you do everything that you can do at home?' (page 15). Discuss the boy's comment. What is your favourite kind of holiday?

6. Make a list of all the things that the boy does not like about his home. What things annoy you most at home? – for example, sharing a room, not being allowed to watch your favourite television programmes, your sisters' friends?

7. Why does the boy think that in the English lesson the teacher will most likely ask one of the girls to recite the poem?

8. Write the letter that Mr Garnett sends to the boy's mother, persuading her to let her son go camping. What sort of information needs to be included?

9. Why does the mother decide to let her son go to the camp? In what ways is this a sacrifice for her?

10. What aspects of the teachers' behaviour in the story do you find realistic or unrealistic? Compare them with Gaffer Roberts (page 66).

11. Why does the boy not enjoy his time at camp? In what ways is the holiday not like he thought it would be?

12. What sort of person do you consider Gordon Barraclough to be?

13. How does the mother embarrass her son when she visits the camp?

14. Why, do you think, does the mother not guess that her son is unhappy when she visits?

15. Imagine you are the boy. Write two letters to your mother, one saying how well things are going in the camp (disguising all the bad things), the second saying how awful everything is (forgetting the good points).

16. From your reading of this story, write a character description of Norbert Lightowler. Look at what he says and does, and at what others say about him.

17. Write the boy's diary for his second week at camp. Set it out with an entry for each day. Think up a series of adventures the boys might have been involved in.

18. Write a story in which a holiday goes wrong from beginning to end.

19. Write about any school journeys or camps you have been on. Include details of the highlights and the worst moments of the holiday.

20. A day at school when *almost* everything goes wrong – almost, but not quite! Write a story on this subject.

Further Reading
Through their stories many writers tell us – directly and indirectly – about when they were children. You might find it interesting to read and compare *The Fib and other stories* by George Layton with Robert Leeson's book *Harold and Bella, Jammy and Me*. Some lively memories of childhood can also be found in *The Goalkeeper's Revenge* by Bill Naughton, *Quite Early One Morning* by Dylan Thomas, and *Summer's End* by Archie Hill.

Harold and Bella

These are two more short stories which have their origins in an author's childhood; they will probably have reminded you of things which have happened to you and your own friends. And, as Robert Leeson reveals, he tries out his stories by telling them to children before he comes to publish them.

I owe these stories to two lots of people. My friends and others that I knew in my home town in the North West of England in the days before the Second World War. Each character is made up of two or three 'real' people; each tale grew out of things that happened or could have happened.

And I owe them to thousands of young people in schools and libraries who heard the stories long before they were published.

(Robert Leeson)

Harold

1. Can you think of various reasons why the rest of the gang put up with Harold?
2. What picture do you have of the children's homes from the details given at the beginning of the story?
3. What does the author mean in writing: 'when Mr Marconi did arrive round our way'? (page 27).
4. What do you think 'Ovaltineys' and 'Joe the Sanpic Man' refer to?
5. What is Bella's attitude towards Harold and Jammy discussing the wireless?
6. Why does Harold's mum say the word *settee* 'a bit louder' (page 29) when all the neighbours are gathered in her front room?
7. What do we learn about the quality of the wireless from the phrase 'Just atmospherics'? Which sentence in the following paragraph suggests similar sound quality?
8. When Jammy's mother invites everyone round for Saturday tea, why does Harold's mother look 'a bit peeved'? And why does Jammy look green at that moment?
9. When Harold is sitting down in Jammy's kitchen why does he have 'a fat grin on his face' to begin with?

103

10. How does Jammy win his bet? Do you think his father knew about the bet?
11. Harold's family always seem to have the latest gadgets. If they were living today, which household things would they be likely to have to stay ahead of their neighbours? What might be the latest gadgets for the home in the year 2030?
12. Find examples in the story which tell you that the story is set in the 1930s. Find out which Royal Wedding is referred to in the tale. You will probably need to look in a library reference book.

Bella

13. Why do you think the author put the little verse about Adam and Eve at the beginning of the story? How does it connect with the action?
14. 'Her parents christened her Dorabella. They were always doing things like that' (page 32). What does this tell us about Bella's parents?
15. What do we learn about the type of school the children attended from the description on page 32?
16. Why do the children not enjoy Sundays?
17. Explain why the parents do not approve of the children going to the Old River. Discuss places where your parents do not like you to go. Describe them if you've been!
18. Where does the word *tow-path* originate?
19. In what way is *Gorse* Hill important to the storyline?
20. Why does Harold not want Bella to come swimming?
21. Which phrase indicates that the gang all ran very quickly to escape the Constable?
22. Why does Bella play the trick on Harold? What clues are there in the story which suggest that Bella *is* playing a trick?

Harold and Bella

23. Which parts of the stories do you find particularly amusing? In what ways does Robert Leeson create a very informal, anecdotal style of storytelling?

24. What sort of picture do you get of the children's parents? Look carefully at what they say and do in both stories. Which family would you rather belong to and why?
25. What qualities does each member of the gang bring to the group? How do you think Jammy got his name? Write a short description of each of the children.
26. How would you compare Bella with the girl in *Equal Rights?*
27. Make up another couple of adventures which involve Harold, Bella, Jammy and Me. You could write these either as a play or a short story.
28. Write a description of someone you know who, like Harold, is always boasting. Mention an occasion when the boasting backfired.
29. Write a short story about a favourite haunt – perhaps a den, a stream, an adventure playground – and an unusual, amusing or memorable incident which you saw take place there.
30. In playing tricks children can be very cruel to each other. Discuss examples of this you can remember. Have you ever been the planner or victim of an unpleasant trick? Write about it.

Further Reading
If you want to find out how Jammy actually *did* get his name or about other adventures the gang had in the town of Tarcroft, then try and read *Harold and Bella, Jammy and Me* from which these two stories have been selected. Other books by Robert Leeson which you may already know or like to read: *The Demon Bike Rider, Challenge in the Dark, The Third Class Genie, It's My Life, Grange Hill Rules – OK?, Grange Hill Goes Wild* and *Grange Hill For Sale.*

How the Tortoise Became

This story belongs to a well-known collection entitled *How the Whale Became.* Just how human beings, animals and Nature were created or have evolved has been the subject of endless discussion and writing throughout history (contrast the myths of the Ancient Greeks), and many writers, like Ted Hughes, have offered unusual and amusing accounts of the Creation. 'To begin with, all the creatures were pretty much alike – very different from what they are now. They had no idea what they were going

105

to become.' Thus Ted Hughes opens his volume on the beginnings of the animal world. Torto's tale concerns the origins of his name, while in other stories the author writes entertainingly, and with great invention, about how the unique qualities and characters of different animals were first formed and developed – from the owl and the hare to the whale and the elephant.

1. Why is God very pleased with the way he has made Elephant?
2. Why is Torto able to escape so easily from God's workshop?
3. What is the first thing Torto does after escaping?
4. Why is Torto such a swift runner?
5. Explain the reason the other creatures do not admire Torto, even though he wins all the races.
6. 'The other animals are snobs' (page 40). Do you agree with Torto? Do you feel they treat him badly?
7. How do the animals force Torto to change his mind about having a skin?
8. When Torto first gets his skin in what ways is life 'perfect for him' (page 42)? Which creature in the wild today is *really* able to take off its skin?
9. How do the animals behave towards Torto when he loses the race, compared with their reactions when he always won?
10. How do they change Torto's name to tortoise? Think of other creatures who may have got their name in a similar way – for example, croc-o-dile, kan-ga-roo, chim-pan-zee. Write the tale of how they won their name.
11. What sort of character does Torto seem to have? Do you think he changes at all in the course of the story?
12. Three animals – Porcupine, Yak and Sloth – comment on Torto's lack of a skin when he first appears. Why do you think Ted Hughes selects these particular creatures? Comment on their distinctive skins.
13. How many different creatures are mentioned in the story?
14. If you were God looking down on all the animals you had created, which ones would you be especially pleased with and why?
15. Reread the opening three paragraphs of the story. Now make a list of as many creatures as you can think of, under

the following headings:

made on a cold day	made in the rain
made on a hot day	made at night
made in the snow	made during the day

made when God was tired and running out of ideas
made when God was trying to be original
(Some creatures may appear in more than one list, of course.)

16. What is the famous Aesop Fable about the tortoise and the hare? Compare it with the events in Ted Hughes's tale.
17. Choose any animal you admire and write the story of its creation. Try to make it original and, perhaps, amusing.
18. There is a celebrated novel called *Metamorphosis* (find out what this word means) in which a man wakes up one morning to find himself turned into a giant insect. The story is then told by the insect. Imagine you are one of the animals in *How the Tortoise Became*: tell what happens to Torto from your viewpoint.
    Or: Imagine you and your friends wake up one day to find yourselves turned into different animals: write a story entitled *A Day In The Life Of* . . . .
19. Different peoples and cultures throughout history have had their own stories about creation. You might like to start a project which compares the various creation myths. Here are some ideas to get you started:

Creation Myths

The Indian Myth of Creation

At first there was no earth and sky; there were only two great eggs. But they were no ordinary eggs for they were soft and shone like gold. As the eggs went round in space they collided and broke open. From one half came the earth and from the other half came the sky. The sky took the earth to be his wife. But the earth was too big for the sky to hold in his arms so he said to her, 'Though you are my wife you are bigger than I. Make yourself smaller.' The earth accordingly made herself smaller and as she became smaller the mountains and valleys were formed. And the earth and the sky were married and made every kind of tree and grass and all living creatures.

107

The Egyptian Myth of Creation
Long ago there was nothing but sea and darkness. One day a flower grew out of the sea. The flower opened to reveal a scarab beetle which gave off light. And so the darkness became light. The beetle changed into a man called Ra. Ra was king of the universe. Ra was lonely so he spat out a son called Shu and a daughter called Tefnut. One day Ra lost his children in the sea. He searched for them and when he at last found them he cried for joy. From out of his tears, men grew. That is why in the Egyptian language the word for 'man' is the same as the word for 'tear'.

The Babylonian Myth of Creation
Babylonia was an ancient kingdom in Southern Mesopotamia. It lay between the rivers Tigris and Euphrates. This country is now called Iraq. The Babylonians believed that their world was created when a good god called Marduk captured an evil goddess called Tiamet. He trapped her in a net and then strangled her. Marduk cut Tiamet's body in two. From the top half he made the skies and the bottom half became the Earth. After this, everything that was good in life was thought to have been caused by Marduk. The evil and disasters that happened were blamed on Tiamet. Just as Marduk and Tiamet fought, so men will always struggle between leading a good life and leading a bad life.

Further Reading
Ted Hughes is one of our most famous living poets and has written quite a lot of poetry and prose especially for children. Perhaps his best-known book is the fabulous tale of *The Iron Man;* you may also like to read his intriguing short story *The Tigerboy* (available in *The Storyteller 2*, edited by Barrett and Morpurgo) and a volume of plays *The Coming of the Kings*. His collections of poetry for children include: *Meet My Folks!*, *Season Songs*, *Moon-Bells*, and *Under The North Star*.

In The Middle of The Night

If we think about our own lives there is rarely anything remarkable about them: most days are filled with predictable events and meeting our friends, neighbours and those we work

with. Yet even the humdrum of everyday life can be made to
seem interesting and exciting in the hands of observant and
skilful writers. Philippa Pearce made up eight stories about
'ordinary' people's ordinary lives and called them simply *What
The Neighbours Did*, and it was in that collection that *In The
Middle of The Night* was first published. Straightforwardly told,
with a keen eye for tiny details and an awareness of children's
inner fears and excitements, the author gives us a tale full of
humour and drama, with a wry twist to end. For those who
have sisters and brothers it will probably remind them of
particular adventures in the home that have happened without
parents ever *really* knowing the whole truth.

1. On which night of the week does the story take place?
2. In the opening paragraphs (pages 45–6) how does the author
   create both a funny scene and a sense of battle between
   Charlie and the fly?
3. Why does Charlie think the fly is actually in his ear? At
   which point in the narrative does he think it has gone?
4. What do you understand by the sentence, 'Wilson turned
   over very slowly like a seal in water' (page 46)?
5. What are the mother's and father's reactions to Charlie's tale
   about the fly?
6. Why does Floss make no sound as Charlie creeps downstairs?
7. Why does Margaret, in particular, not want to be discovered
   by her parents?
8. Which phrase tells us that Margaret has been sitting in the
   hall for quite a time?
9. What do you think goes through Alison's mind when she
   first comes upon Charlie and Margaret in the kitchen?
10. What do we learn about Alison's character from the sentence
    'In such a way must Napoleon have viewed a battlefield
    before victory' (page 50)?
11. Write down the reasons why each of the four children came
    to be in the kitchen in the middle of the night.
12. Judging from clues in the story, how long would you guess
    each of the children are in the kitchen?
13. Explain why Alison tells Wilson that the potato-cakes are
    paradise-cakes.

14. In what various ways does Alison show herself to be the eldest child in the family?
15. 'Wilson liked talking even if no one would listen' (page 53). What do we learn about him from this description? Is there anyone in your family or amongst your friends of whom the same might be said?
16. What is your reaction to the way the story ends? Are there any signs that the parents have guessed what has really happened?
17. How would your mother or father react to an incident similar to the one in this story? Describe an occasion when this sort of thing has happened in your family.
18. Using the same characters and setting, write another story when Charlie is awoken at night.
19. Invent a plot about you and your brothers or sisters (or friends) doing something behind your parents' back. How do you hide the truth? Write the events as a short story or as a play.
20. Write a story about a secret and grand midnight feast, the events leading up to it, the preparations you make, and perhaps something or someone giving you away at the end.

Further Reading
Philippa Pearce is another established writer for children; try to read *What The Neighbours Did* and her other collection of short stories *The Shadow-Cage*, which has ten chilling tales about the supernatural. Her novels include the famous *Tom's Midnight Garden, A Dog So Small, The Elm Street Lot* and *The Battle of Bubble and Squeak.*

The Monkey's Paw

In a recent survey of children's reading habits the most popular kind of fiction enjoyed by eleven and twelve year-olds proved to be stories about ghosts, spooks and the supernatural. What is it that makes most of us so fascinated by this subject? Perhaps it is because the question of whether there is life beyond this earth is the one that all the wonders of modern science have still left unexplained. Certainly *The Monkey's Paw* is a classic tale of the supernatural, with all the ingredients of an eerie house in an out-of-the-way place, strange visitors, an unusual talisman, a rising from the grave, and a final, chilling twist. But the story must also make us think long and hard about the role of Fate in our lives and about what someone once called 'the vanity of human wishes'.

1. What sort of atmosphere is created in the opening lines which is important for the whole story? How does the author do this? Contrast the mood at the end of the story.

2. How are we told that Mr White and Sergeant-Major Morris are old friends?

3. Why is Morris so welcome to the White household?

4. What is Morris's immediate reaction to mention of the monkey's paw?

5. What things does Morris say and do which make the paw seem sinister?

6. Explain what Mrs White means when she says the tales about the paw sound like the 'Arabian Nights'. Find out some of the stories of the 'Arabian Nights'.

7. Why does Morris look alarmed when Mrs White suggests they wish her 'four pairs of hands'?

8. Which line spoken by Herbert (page 59) is a macabre prediction of the outcome of the story?

9. Before the White family go to bed for the night what signs are there that good will not come of the first wish? Do you think that Herbert believes in the tales Morris has told? Look carefully for clues in the text.

10. Why does the stranger listen to Mrs White 'in a preoccupied fashion' (page 60)?

11. 'Badly hurt ... but he is not in any pain' (page 61). Explain how this comment has two meanings for Mrs White.

12. What suggests to you that the visitor from Maw and Meggins is perhaps used to breaking this kind of news? Look at the 'official' words he uses – what do they mean (page 61)?

13. Describe how the author creates a sense of tension in the story, from the point when the second wish is made. Study page 64 carefully.

14. Why is there a time gap between the second wish being made and coming true?

15. What is Mr White's 'third and last wish'? Why does he make it?
16. 'Morris said the things happened so naturally that you might think it was only coincidence' (page 60). In what way does this come true in the story?
17. Why do the White family ignore all Sergeant-Major Morris's warnings about the monkey's paw?
18. 'The first man had his three wishes. I don't know what the first two were, but the third was for death. That's how I got the paw' (page 57). Write the story which led to Morris getting the paw.
19. Morris says that the fakir who put a spell on the paw 'wanted to show that fate ruled people's lives and that those who interfered with it did so to their sorrow' (page 56). Do you think Fate rules our lives? Discuss the difference between Fate and Free Will. In what ways do the two tales, *Swollen-Foot* and *The Outside Chance*, connect with the fakir's words?
20. Continue the story of *The Monkey's Paw*, imagining that the third wish did *not* come true.
21. You are a local reporter and go along to interview Mr White about his son's death. Write the story from Mr White's point of view; remember you need to use the 'I' form of narration (see notes above).
22. Mr and Mrs White have just told their story to another visitor. She decides to have three wishes. Write the next episode of *The Monkey's Paw*. You could write this as a play, taping it afterwards complete with sound effects!

Further Reading

W. W. Jacobs lived in Victorian times and wrote many stories about long-shoremen, barge crews, night-watchmen and others who earned their living by the sea and boats but who were not ocean-going seamen. *The Monkey's Paw* first appeared in a collection entitled *The Lady of the Barge* and may well have had its origins in a tale told by sailors returned from the mystical East. Other recommended anthologies of the supernatural: *Ghosts* edited by Aidan Chambers; *Ghostly and Ghastly* edited by Barbara Ireson; *Thrillers, Chillers and Killers, A Chilling Collection* and others edited by Helen Hoke.

Gaffer Roberts

Skulker Wheat and Other Stories, from which *Gaffer Roberts* is taken, is a collection which gives a memorable account of life in a small Midlands village in the years just after the Second World War. The title story tells of the sad death of Skulker Wheat after a series of epileptic fits, and the rest of the tales in the volume are told by one of his friends in memory of all the times he, Skulker and the rest of their gang spent together. *Gaffer Roberts* is, then, a sort of flashback story; the 'I' is a boy narrator about eleven years old, but (like George Layton in *The Holiday*) it is also the author John Griffin affectionately recalling his own rural childhood As the stories of these two authors and those of Robert Leeson (*Harold* and *Bella* and *Grange Hill*) remind us, children of every generation, wherever they live, play similar tricks and enjoy much of their fun at the expense of the same old 'enemies' – teachers and parents.

1. How does the writer bring out the funny side of all the family fighting? Why do you think he concentrates on the humour in the situations?
2. What picture do you have of the house this family live in? Look for small details in the opening paragraphs.
3. What does the boy narrator mean when he says: 'I gave him a push – not a hard push, just defensive' (page 67)?
4. When the father falls downstairs, why is it 'a significant moment' for the boy? Can you think of any similar moments that have occurred in your family?
5. Explain the meaning of: 'What used to be a real chase had become a ritual' (page 68).
6. How does the story about the father falling downstairs link up with Gaffer Roberts?
7. What particular things about Gaffer does the narrator not like? What does he find amusing about him?
8. What was rather different about the top class at the village school, compared with the average classroom nowadays?
9. Why is it the Vicar who arrives to tell the class about Gaffer coming out of retirement? Why is he needed to teach?
10. 'We all knew Gaffer's reputation and felt we had to be on our best behaviour' (page 70). How had Gaffer built his

113

reputation over the years? Why are the class able to 'break' him so easily, do you think?

11. Who was and what is Pythagoras (page 70)?

12. Explain what Gaffer means about the difference between 'can' and 'may'. What does this private joke of his tell you about his style of teaching?

13. 'We'll have to find a new goalkeeper for the football team' (page 71). What is the narrator suggesting when he thinks this?

14. Why do the children not 'muck about' with Mrs Armitage when she takes over? What makes pupils play around with certain teachers and not others? Discuss what you consider to be the qualities of a good teacher.

15. 'If you scare people by hitting them then one day they'll be able to get you; it stands to reason' (page 73). Do you agree? Use this comment as a starting point for a story of your own.

16. Write a full character description of Gaffer Roberts. Study what he says and how he behaves, and what other people think about him.

17. Rewrite the classroom scenes with Gaffer from *his* point of view. Remember to start with 'I' in telling the story.

18. Describe an occasion in your house when your mother or father have been very angry because of something you have done. Do you have a special place of retreat like the boy in the story?

19. Discuss the types of practical jokes you and your friends have played on teachers.

20. Write a story or a short play in which a strict teacher and a tough pupil come into conflict with each other.

21. Write on one or more of the following:

> A day in the life of a new teacher
> Memories of my favourite teacher
> Memories of junior school
> My first week at secondary school

Further Reading

John Griffin has written another collection of stories, *Behind the Goal*. The stories of Stan Barstow, Bill Naughton and Keith Waterhouse offer other fascinating pictures of growing up, and some are available in *First Choice* (edited by Michael

Marland). You might also like to compare the country child-
hoods in H. E. Bates's short stories and Laurie Lee's popular
novel, *Cider with Rosie*, with Farrukh Dondy's city scenes in
Come to Mecca.

The Outside Chance

The success of this tale lies in a straightforward, timeless plot
which continues to haunt us long after we have read the final
paragraphs. As when we have finished reading *The Monkey's
Paw* or *Swollen-Foot* we are likely to begin wondering about
coincidence, Fate and what the gods have stored up for each and
every one of us. It is also worth looking back over the text in
some detail to help you with writing your own short stories: *The
Outside Chance* has a small number of characters who are
described briefly and clearly; one event leads naturally – or
rather supernaturally – to the next; while the first-person narration, short paragraphs and simple but effective vocabulary all
make for easy reading.

1. Why had the young man left his mother and father?
2. What are his feelings towards his father at the start of the
   story?
3. What does the narrator mean when he says: 'if only I could
   get out of the rut' (page 75)?
4. Explain the ideas behind the phrase: 'As if there was a gap in
   the news' (page 75).
5. Why did the young man not stop to think why 'tomorrow's
   paper' had come into his hands?
6. Explain what 30–1 and 50–1 mean if you go into a betting
   shop.
7. Why does he place his bets at different shops?
8. How does the young man guess his father is dead before the
   telegram arrives?
9. Discuss the similarities between this story and *The Monkey's
   Paw*.
10. If you picked up 'tomorrow's paper' today, what things in it
    would immediately tell you that it was a jump ahead? Write a
    story based on this idea of receiving tomorrow's paper today.

11. The factory disaster in Selby is mentioned in the 'Stop Press'. Where do you find the 'Stop Press' in a newspaper and what is it? Collect some actual examples from this section of any newspaper.

12. Imagine you are a reporter on the newspaper at the centre of this story. Prepare some questions to ask the young man about these strange events. Write up the interview you have with him.

13. 'If you want something really badly, you'll probably get it. But you'll probably get it in a way you don't expect' (page 74). What do you think? Write your own story with this statement as either a starting or finishing point.

14. Further essay titles: The Outside Chance
    A strange twist of fate in the family
    If only I could get a thousand quid
    A chance to see into the future

Further Reading
Jan Carew has written other stories about the supernatural in the volume *Save The Last Dance For Me*.

The Wild Geese

This tale is from a marvellous collection of stories about childhood on a farm during the 1950s. 'The lands of Kincaple' referred to in the opening line are actually on the east coast of Scotland in the county of Fife – 'shaped like the head of a dog, looking out, ears pricked and alert, over the North Sea'. This area is also the home of the author Emil Pacholek; clearly based on his own young days, the collection offers a richly detailed and sharply evocative picture of a closely-knit rural community, undergoing a period of change brought about by the increasing mechanisation of farm life. Robbie is the central character in all the stories and through him the reader can relive the great Open Golf Championship at St Andrews in July 1955, the local harvest celebrations, the exploits of the visiting tinks, and an unforgettable day's pig-killing. The particular enjoyment in reading *The Wild Geese* comes from the way the author enables us to share and identify with the invention, daring and excitement of the boys' plan, its initial success, and final uncovering by 'the Local

Police Force himself!' And as with so many short stories, there is a memorable concluding twist.

1. 'The plan! That was all that mattered! That was all they thought about ...' (page 78). At which point in the first pages of the story did you guess the details of the plan?
2. Why do Robbie and McPhee whisper when they are all alone building their hide?
3. Why do you think the boys particularly wanted to catch the geese?
4. What do we know about McPhee's background?
5. In which season of the year does the story take place? Pick out some of the farming details which tell you.
6. Which details reveal that Dauve enjoys and is very good at his work?
7. Explain the 'strange look' that comes over Dauve when Robbie mentions tractors replacing horses on the farm (page 83).
8. Why does Robbie smile 'a secret little smile to himself' as he is eating his stewed hare?
9. Why does Robbie make tea for his mother that evening? What shows that he is not used to doing this little job?
10. Discuss how the writer creates the night atmosphere on pages 86–7.
11. How does the author highlight the tension and sense of waiting when the boys are in their hide? Look at the words and sentences on pages 88–9; discuss the way the action is gradually built up to the climax when the boys capture their prey.
12. 'It seemed to the two boys that there was a sort of unruliness creeping in' (page 89). Explain their thoughts at this point.
13. Why does Robbie decide to put the goose straight onto the kitchen table when he reaches home?
14. Why is Sergeant Baxter described as 'the Local Police Force himself'?
15. In what ways does the policeman hint that he would like a drink before he leaves?
16. What has happened at the very end of the story? Why does Robbie look on 'like a doomed rabbit'? Write an extra, final paragraph to *The Wild Geese*.

17. There is a similar scene involving diluted whisky in one of Charles Dickens' novels, *Great Expectations*. Find a copy of the novel and look in chapter 4. Compare the reactions of Robbie and the Sergeant with those of Pip and Uncle Pumblechook in *Great Expectations*.
18. Do you believe that the whisky could have doped the geese? Read *The Champion of the World*, a short story by Roald Dahl in which poachers catch pheasants by drugging them with sleeping pills. Compare the setting, events and ending with those in *The Wild Geese*.
19. Compile a list of all the Scottish dialect words used in the story – for example: bothy, skelp, wee dram.
20. Which details in the story suggest that it is set some years ago?
21. Write a 'police report' of the night's events, as Sergeant Baxter would have entered it in his records.
22. Write another adventure involving Robbie and McPhee in 'the lands of Kincaple'.
23. Have you ever built a den or a hide like the boys in the story? Write a description of it and an incident which took place there.
24. Make up a short story about a night adventure which goes well until the very last moment . . . when disaster occurs.

Further Reading
If you have enjoyed this story it is well worth reading the whole collection *Robbie* by Emil Pacholek. You might like to contrast stories from different countries or regions. Try *Short Stories from Wales*, *Short Stories from America*, *Short Stories from Ireland* in Wheaton's Literature for Life series.

Further ideas for group and individual work

+ Which of the stories did you enjoy most? Give reasons. Write a short review of your favourite story from this collection which will encourage others to want to read it. Try to mention something about the plot, characters, setting, themes and author's style (see pages 93–6).

+ Which characters did you like or identify with? Write your own story in which you bring together characters from different stories in this volume: for example, Bella and Alison (from *In The Middle of The Night*) and the girl from *Equal Rights*.

+ What are your reactions to the ways the stories end? If you don't like one of the endings, try rewriting or acting out a different conclusion; this may, of course, change the message or overall mood of the tale.

+ Take the last lines of any of the stories and write some scenes that might follow on. As an experiment, you could try and capture something of the original author's particular style of writing.

+ There are several families presented in these stories. Which household, if any, would you enjoy living in and why? What do you think of the way the parents and children behave towards one another – is it realistic?

+ From your reading of certain stories in the volume, what would you say are the important ingredients to include when creating a tale of the supernatural?

+ Some of the authors have tried to bring out the humour of events and of characters. Look back over the stories and discuss where and how they have succeeded for you in doing this.

+ Jan Carew in *The Outside Chance* uses the first-person 'I' narration, while W. W. Jacobs in *The Monkey's Paw* has a third-person narrator observing the action from the outside. Which type of narration is used in each of these eleven stories? What seem to you the advantages and disadvantages of the different narrative standpoints? Try writing your own version of any of the stories by having an alternative narrator from the one used in the original.

+ Some of the stories have obvious regional settings – *The Wild Geese* and *Gaffer Roberts*, for example – and their authors employ local vocabulary. Make a list of examples of regional dialect from the stories; compare them with words in your own local dialect.

+ As well as telling a story writers are often concerned to make a point about a certain subject. What seem to you to be some of the underlying ideas of the authors in this volume? Has any of

119

the stories changed your opinions about something, or made
you think about a subject you have not considered before?

+ It is an interesting and challenging assignment to try and
devise an acting script out of an already published story. Many
writers need to do this regularly when they turn a short story
or novel into a film, a radio play or television series. Look at
the following example, taken from *Equal Rights* (page 4):

Scene   A paper-shop
Characters Girl
           Bobby
           The shop-keeper

The shop-keeper is leaning on the counter as the girl, wheeling a
push-chair, enters the shop.

GIRL   Afternoon. We've come down for Mr Dawson's
papers, haven't we, Bobby?

SHOP-KEEPER (*surprised*) Mr Dawson's? Number twenty-nine? '

GIRL   Yes, please.

SHOP-KEEPER (*nodding at Bobby*) Are you . . .?

GIRL   That's right.

He lifts out some papers from under the counter.

SHOP-KEEPER (*fingering the magazines*) Oh, look. I've got last
month's *Pop Today* left over. (*smiling*) You can
have it if you like, with my compliments.

GIRL   Thanks a lot.

SHOP-KEEPER (*quickly*) And about that job. Stupid of me, I'd got
it wrong. What did I say – *four* pounds a week?

GIRL   I think so. It sounded like a four.

SHOP-KEEPER How daft can you get? It was those kids in the
corner. Took my attention off. Of course it's *five*,
you realise that. Have you spoken to your dad yet?

GIRL   No, not yet.

SHOP-KEEPER (*relaxing*) Are you still interested?

GIRL   Yes. Thank you very much.

This is quite simple to do. Choose your story and read through it
a few times. Work through the text slowly, remembering to put
the speaker's name in the margin, and everything she or he

actually *says* on to the main part of your page. You do not need to put in any speech marks. The information about the speakers' reactions, feelings or movements which are given in the story need to be changed into stage directions: for example – 'You should have seen the man's face' can become simply: (*surprised*). Write the short directions in brackets before a character's actual words. Longer stage directions need to be written out separately in the text, and you will probably have to edit and leave out some of the author's original detail. Remember also to use the present tense: for example, 'He *lifts* out some papers. ...'

Now try turning any bit of action from one of the stories in this volume into a playscript. When you have finished tape it or present it to the rest of your group.

Note – start with something quite straightforward with just two or three speakers, before attempting a more complicated scene. It also helps to choose a story in which there is plenty of dialogue! Some possible starting points:

a. The classroom scene in *The Holiday* (pages 20–2)
b. The kitchen feast in *In The Middle of The Night* (pages 49–52)
c. The evening of Sergeant-Major Morris's visit in *The Monkey's Paw* (pages 55–8)
d. The classroom scene in *Gaffer Roberts* (pages 70–2)

Further Reading

Note: Where a book is published in both hardback and paperback editions, details of paperback only are given.

Equal Rights

Bernard Ashley, *The Trouble with Donovan Croft*, Puffin Books, 1977; *Terry on the Fence*, Puffin, 1978; *All My Men*, Puffin, 1979; *Break in the Sun*, Puffin, 1981; *Dodgem*, Julia MacRae Books, 1981; *A Kind of Wild Justice*, Puffin, 1982

Swollen-Foot

Kenneth McLeish, *The Robe of Blood*, Knockouts Series, Longman, 1976

Leon Garfield and Edward Blishen, *The God Beneath the Sea*, Kestrel Books, 1976; *The Golden Shadow*, Kestrel Books, 1978

The Holiday

George Layton, *Northern Childhood: The Balaclava Story* and *The Fib and Other Stories*, Knockouts Series, Longman, 1979

Bill Naughton, *The Goalkeeper's Revenge and Other Stories*, New Windmill Series, Heinemann Educational Books, 1967

Dylan Thomas, *Quite Early One Morning*, Dent, 1967

Archie Hill, *Summer's End*, Wheaton, 1979

Harold and Bella

Robert Leeson, *Harold and Bella, Jammy and Me*, Armada Books, 1980; *The Demon Bike Rider*, Armada 1977; *Challenge in the Dark*, Collins, 1978; *The Third Class Genie*, Armada, 1975; *It's My Life*, Collins, 1980; *Grange Hill Rules – OK?*, Armada, 1979; *Grange Hill Goes Wild*, Armada, 1980; *Grange Hill for Sale*, Armada, 1981

How the Tortoise Became

Ted Hughes, *How the Whale Became and Other Stories*, Puffin, 1971; *The Iron Man: A Story in Five Nights*, Faber, 1971; 'The Tigerboy', in *The Storyteller, Book 2*, ed. Morpurgo and Barrett, Ward Lock Educational, 1980; *The Coming of the Kings and Other Plays*, Faber, 1970; *Meet My Folks!*, Puffin, 1977; *Season Songs*, Faber, 1976; *Moon-bells and Other Poems*, Chatto, 1978; *Under the North Star*, Faber, 1981

In The Middle of The Night

Philippa Pearce, *What the Neighbours Did and Other Stories*, Puffin, 1975; *The Shadow-Cage*, Puffin, 1978; *Tom's Midnight Garden*, Puffin, 1976; *A Dog So Small*, Puffin, 1970; *The Elm Street Lot*, Puffin, 1980; *The Battle of Bubble and Squeak*, Puffin, 1980

The Monkey's Paw

The Monkey's Paw from *The Supernatural*, ed. Adams and Jones, Anchor Books, Chambers, 1979

Aidan Chambers, *Haunted Houses*, Piccolo, 1971; *I Want to Get Out*, Topliners, Macmillan, 1971; *The Book of Ghosts and Hauntings*, Longman, 1973;

Barbara Ireson, *Ghostly and Ghastly*, Beaver Books, Hamlyn, 1977

Helen Hoke, ed., *Thrillers, Chillers and Killers*, Dent, 1979; *A Chilling Collection*, Dent, 1980

Gaffer Roberts

John Griffin, *Skulker Wheat*, New Windmill Series, Heinemann Educational Books, 1979; *Behind the Goal*, Knockouts, Longman, 1979

M. Marland, ed., *First Choice*, Longman, 1971

Laurie Lee, *Cider with Rosie*, Penguin, 1970

Farrukh Dondy, *Come to Mecca and Other Stories*, Armada, Collins, 1978

The Outside Chance

Jan Carew, *Save the Last Dance for Me*, Knockouts, Longman, 1976; *Stranger than Tomorrow*, Knockouts, Longman, 1976; *You Can't Explain Everything*, Knockouts, Longman 1976; *The Man Who Came Back*, Knockouts, Longman, 1979; *House of Fear*, Knockouts, Longman, 1981

Anita Jackson, *Bennet Manor*, Spirals Series, Hutchinson, 1976; *The Ear*, Spirals Series, Hutchinson, 1976

The Wild Geese

Emil Pacholek, *Robbie*, André Deutsch, 1980
Elias, ed. *Short Stories from Wales*. Wheaton, 1978
Jenkins, ed., *Short Stories from America*, Wheaton, 1978
Calthorp, ed., *Short Stories from Ireland*, Wheaton, 1979

Acknowledgments

The editor and publishers wish to thank the following for permission to reprint the short stories:

Bernard Ashley for *Equal Rights*:
Longman Group Ltd. for *Swollen-Foot* from *The Robe of Blood* by Kenneth McLeish:
Longman Group Ltd. for *The Holiday* from *Northern Childhood: The Balaclava Story* by George Layton:
William Collins Sons and Co. Ltd. (Fontana Paperbacks) for *Harold* and *Bella* from *Harold and Bella, Jammy and Me* by Robert Leeson:
Faber and Faber Ltd. for *How the Tortoise Became* from *How the Whale Became* by Ted Hughes:
Penguin Books Ltd. for *In The Middle of The Night* from *What the Neighbours Did and Other Stories* by Philippa Pearce, published by Penguin Books Ltd., © Philippa Pearce, 1959, 1967, 1969, 1972.
William Heinemann Ltd. for *Gaffer Roberts* from *Skulker Wheat* by John Griffin:
Longman Group Ltd. for *The Outside Chance* from *Save the Last Dance for Me* by Jan Carew:
The Society of Authors as the literary representative of the Estate of W. W. Jacobs for *The Monkey's Paw* by W. W. Jacobs:
André Deutsch for *The Wild Geese* from *Robbie* by Emil Pacholek, published by André Deutsch, 1980.